Turquoise
PARADE

For information, address Bamzyl Books, 7145 Mile Road, Sun Prairie, WI 53590

Written and compiled by Lori Lipsky

Cover, typesetting, and e-book design by Michelle Rayburn missionandmedia.com

Benjamin Franklin, *Autobiography: Poor Richard Letters,* (New York: D. Appleton, 1904) 237.

Scripture quotations are from the *ESV® Bible (The Holy Bible, English Standard Version®),* Copyright © 2001 by Crossway, a publishing ministry of Good News Publishers. Used by permission. All rights reserved.

2022 First Edition

to Mark

Turquoise PARADE

Stories

Lori Lipsky

BAMZYL BOOKS

Contents

Give the Dog a Bath

Their marriage counselor advised the young couple to do more things together. He suggested they begin with household tasks such as emptying the dishwasher, shopping for groceries, and cleaning the bathroom. He also gave them the assignment to say thank you and make affirming remarks to each other at least twice a day.

Neither Tilly nor Logan liked to bathe the dog. Since the groomer charged ninety dollars each visit, they decided to do it themselves this time. Luckily, the apartment bathtub could hold their dog. Tilly's sister promised to come over with her tools to trim his nails after Snoogy's bath.

Logan attempted to lure the dog into the bathroom. Tilly sat on the toilet seat, her hands busy holding the baby. For several minutes, Logan used what her mother had always called an outdoor voice. Tilly covered the baby's ears with her hands, and using *her* outdoor voice, she said, "You could try peanut butter."

Logan couldn't resist telling her the trick wouldn't work before he walked to their tiny kitchen to put some peanut butter in a small dish.

Snoogy followed Logan and the dish of peanut butter into the bathroom. As soon as the pup's tail cleared the doorway, Tilly stood and closed the bathroom door.

Once Snoogy realized he had no escape, he forgot about peanut butter for a moment and planted his eighty-pound body against the door. Logan used both hands to nudge him toward the tub, but Snoogy refused to budge.

Earlier, Tilly had filled the tub with four or five inches of water after securing a non-slip bathmat in place. Her friend had suggested that, perhaps, Snoogs didn't like the tub because of its slippery surface.

"Logan, you could apply swipes of peanut butter around the upper inside edge of the far side of the tub," Tilly suggested. "Then Snoogs would need to step into the bathtub to reach the peanut butter with his tongue."

"That won't work," Logan said. He tried again to pull Snoogy toward the tub, but Snoogs resisted. He sat down and started to whine.

"Be patient and let the peanut butter do its magic," Tilly said.

Logan expressed doubt using his indoor voice, but soon he followed Tilly's advice and sat on the side of the tub to wait.

After pretending to be disinterested for two minutes, Snoogy sniffed. He stood up and moseyed over to the tub. He stretched his nose toward the peanut butter on the far side of the tub but couldn't quite reach it with his tongue. Snoogy sniffed and sniffed and finally succumbed. He lifted his front legs one at a time and stepped in.

Logan tried to lift the dog's back legs. Distracted by the peanut butter, he acquiesced. As Snoogs licked at the peanut butter, Logan went to work, quickly wetting the dog with their shower attachment, then shampooing him. Holding the baby with one arm, Tilly added thin smears of peanut butter to the tub as needed to keep Snoogy distracted.

While he rinsed Snoogy off for the last time, Logan admitted, "The peanut butter was a great idea. I'm not sure what else we would have done."

"Thank you," Tilly said.

Snoogs went over every smudge of peanut butter with his tongue five times. When no more came, he apparently decided his bath was over. He leaped out onto the rug and shook himself dry. Logan wrapped an old towel around Snoogs as fast as he could.

The baby giggled.

Tilly and Logan glanced at each other, their grins expressing delight to hear the sound. Only earlier that week, they'd heard her laugh out loud for the first time.

"He got the baby all wet," Tilly said. "I'm going to put some dry clothes on her before she catches cold. The baby and I think you did a good job, by the way. We can clean this up together after she goes to sleep."

"Thanks," Logan said. After he dried Snoogy some more, he worked on the bathroom mess. By the time his wife returned with their dry baby, Logan had the tub and floor cleaned up. Tilly passed the baby to Logan. She put the dog shampoo and conditioner away, placed the wet towels in the laundry room, and finished tidying while Logan sat on the toilet holding the baby.

Tilly held out her hands. "I'll put her to bed tonight. You took your turn last night."

Logan stood and carried the baby out of the bathroom. He looked back over his shoulder. "Come on. We'll do it together tonight."

Tilly and Logan took their baby into the nursery. Snoogy followed along behind his family, smelling better than he had in a long while.

The Boys in World War II

G randma and I used to watch movies together on Sunday afternoons. She popped popcorn using a pan on her stovetop and Crisco oil. My job was to shake the pan back and forth and back and forth while Grandma put ice cubes in tall glasses and filled them with Royal Crown Cola. When the popcorn began to lift the lid off, Grandma took over. She carried the pop and popcorn into the living room. We'd sit next to each other, and as long as I placed my glass on a coaster on the coffee table, we were allowed to eat in the living room.

Mama would never permit such things at her house. Sometimes Grandma would bake cookies or brownies, and we could eat them in the living room too.

"Don't worry," she would say. "I have all week to vacuum crumbs up. This is my Christy time, and I'm not going to worry about spills and spatters while you're here."

Grandma loved old war movies. They seemed old to me, but they were World War II movie reenactments of battles that took place while she was growing up in a small town in Iowa.

"I know two boys who fought in that actual battle, Christy," she said. "They were in my sister's class. She was five grades ahead of me. Do you know that every single boy in her class went to the war? Every single one. Would you believe, one boy was a star of the basketball team, and two soldiers came to the high school one day near the end of the game. They escorted him right from the basketball game and walked him out. That's how he entered the war."

She tossed a piece of popcorn in the air and caught it with her mouth. I tried four times before one finally hit the goal. Grandma gave me a high five.

"Nobody knew they could do such a thing until it happened right in front of our eyes. I was in the stands that night. You don't forget something like that. I think he might have been older than the rest. His mama started him late. That probably helped him do better in sports because he was a year older than everyone else."

If it was chilly, Grandma would tell me to fetch the afghan from the hope chest in the guest room. We'd pull the cold blanket over us and nestle together underneath. Pretty soon, instead of us warming the cold blanket, the blanket would be warming us.

"Now who is the actor who plays the general?" she said. "I know, but I can't think of his name. I wish Grandpa were here. He always knew. Fetch that actor book your family gave me for Christmas."

I'd grab the big book of Hollywood actors off the shelf and spend the next commercial break searching the book for the actor Grandma was thinking of. We sometimes were distracted by the photos, but as soon as the movie started again, I'd put the book down and save it for the next commercial. There were no pause buttons, and we couldn't skip the commercials, so we used them for actor research and restroom breaks.

Sometimes Grandma would say to me, "Could you mute that, Christy? If I have to listen to another one of those commercials, I think my brain might fry."

I'd run to the television and turn down the volume, then run back and turn it up when the featured movie came on again. Grandma never knew the luxury of a remote, but she didn't need one when I was around.

When our movie was over, Grandma would wash the dishes, and I'd dry them and put them away. I knew where everything went because I was there most Sunday afternoons. After church, Mama worked at the diner for what she called her pocket money. "Every woman needs some pocket money," she often said. "Especially a woman with two kids."

Daddy loved watching sports with my brother on Sundays. Since I had no interest in any of the games, our regular Sunday afternoon schedule worked out perfectly for all of us. I wouldn't trade my memories of those times with Grandma for anything.

Crosswalk at East Franklin Avenue

According to the letter they received from the city, the street in front of the Muller's modest Tudor home will be under construction for the next eight to ten weeks. Yesterday, workers spent the day tearing the road up. Curbs and everything.

Jerry Muller knows something about construction, having hired remodelers to work on their home several times over the last twenty years. They renovated their kitchen first. After saving for a few years, they hired workers to remodel their primary bathroom. Then their guest bathroom. Jerry knows from hard experience that eight weeks usually means more than three months in the world of construction.

Rex needs his daily walk, and he lets Jerry know it. Neither Rex nor Jerry's wife allow him to forget the walk for even one day, no matter the weather. Jerry's wife didn't want another dog, but she gave in when Jerry committed to all aspects of the new dog's care.

Rex refuses to walk on the new rough texture of the road out front, and Jerry figures it might not be safe for either of them. For the next few months, Jerry needs to take Rex through their backyard to walk along the edge of the frontage road adjacent to their wide lot. After a hundred yards or so on the busy frontage road, he needs to cross East Franklin Avenue at the intersection, escorting Rex to the far side of the eight-lane thoroughfare. Once they cross, plenty of route options await.

Crossing East Franklin, or East Frank as the locals have dubbed it, won't be so bad, he thinks. Jerry reaches the crosswalk and presses the traffic light button. The speed limit of the road is only forty miles per hour, and since it's Sunday, he won't deal with rush-hour traffic.

A minute after Jerry presses the walk button, the light indicates he may proceed. In the dog's eagerness, Rex stays in front of Jerry, within his line of sight. Jerry likes how this makes the task at hand easy. He crosses the first four lanes at a brisk pace. When the light starts to blink, he breaks into a jog. A car facing him at the intersection begins to inch forward, its signal indicating the vehicle wants to turn right, intersecting the crosswalk Jerry now uses.

By the time Jerry passes through the first half of the eighth lane, the car pulls out and passes right behind him, missing his heel by only an inch or two. Jerry actually feels a breeze as the two-ton vehicle crosses right behind him. Jerry stops when he reaches the sidewalk. He takes a good look at the rear of the black SUV. He memorizes the license number and writes a short letter in his head "To whom it may concern" before mentally ripping up the letter and throwing it away, as his therapist had advised some years ago.

The next day, as Jerry crosses the final two lanes of Franklin Avenue, the driver of a blue sports car sits revving his engine. Thankfully, Rex pulls on the leash in front of him. Before Jerry finishes crossing and steps onto the curb, the blue car accelerates, squealing its tires, barely missing Jerry's heels as the driver did the day before. He turns to get the license plate, but the car is already too far away. On the route home, Jerry runs into the same sort of problem at the crosswalk.

"Don't you dare, Gerald Michael!" his wife says. Jerry holds Rex by the leash in one hand and a baseball bat in the other. He tells his wife about the intersection and says he plans to teach the drivers there a thing or two about decency.

"Someone needs to teach these drivers a lesson, or one day soon, somebody who walks slower because of age or health will be crossing, and one of these yahoos will clip their heels. Or if a dog lags behind, it'll get killed."

"You put that bat down, Jerry. If the police haul you away, who will take the trash out around here? And wash the dishes? And who will walk Rex? We need you. Come here." She beckons him with her arm.

He leans the bat against the wall and goes over to his wife and kisses the lips she offers. "I need to do *something*," he says.

"I'd rather you stay out of trouble. Police can spot a bat a mile away. Can't you put some of that fourth-degree-black-belt-martial-arts-stuff to good use? A quick kick would be unexpected and harder to prove than a dent from a baseball bat." Jerry isn't sure if she is teasing or serious.

He drops Rex's leash and runs upstairs to change his shoes and stretch before they head out.

When he reaches the intersection, he is alert and prepared. Jerry jogs with Rex across all eight lanes. The well-dressed woman who waits to turn right lingers at least two seconds after he steps onto the curb before she proceeds. *Finally, a driver with decency*, Jerry thinks.

On the way home, though, a compact car at the intersection inches forward and sneaks out before he is across. Jerry hopes none of the students where he trains are within eyeshot as his quick side kick connects with the rear door of the vehicle cutting close behind him.

Afterward, he immediately collects himself and continues down the sidewalk with Rex. He wonders if he dented the car—he hopes so. The kick and his recovery occurred so fast that he doubts the driver had any idea what happened.

He debates if he'll share his adventure with his wife. Maybe he should spare her the details, he decides. If she ever notices his steel-toed boots and asks him about them, he'll tell her. Until then, it will be his secret. His and Rex's.

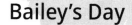

Bailey's Day

T he minute Bailey awakened, she remembered her open schedule. She had nothing planned for the entire day. That never happened.

She had slept an extra hour just because she could. Today belonged to her. No appointments. No responsibilities. No rushing.

Before she even climbed out of bed, she heard herself humming. She hummed all the way to the kitchen. Bailey couldn't remember the last time she'd caught herself humming or singing. What a terrific day it was going to be.

She decided to treat herself to her favorite breakfast food. Usually, she was in too much of a rush to prepare five-minute poached eggs and toast. As she waited for the water to boil, she noticed a text from Margie, who asked if they could chat.

Bailey hesitated before calling. But Margie had mentioned yesterday that she had the day off too. Maybe she was organizing another trivia night. Bailey loved trivia.

"Hey! It's my day off. No work talk allowed," Bailey said.

They both laughed.

"Just let me get this off my chest," Margie said. "You'll never guess what Derrick told me last night about Cherise." She continued without taking a breath. Derrick loved company gossip even more than Margie did—it was important to stay on their good side. Margie kept going, never allowing a break for Bailey to cut in.

Oh no, Bailey thought. *She isn't in one of her delightful moods. She's in one of her cranky, disagreeable moods.* Margie definitely knew how to grumble and moan.

Bailey couldn't stand ten-minute eggs. As soon as her timer went off, she walked close to it and bent down so the phone was as near as possible to the noisy timer. The trick seemed to help. Margie lost her train of thought for a moment, and Bailey was able to sneak into the conversation. She needed to get off this call before Margie and her incessant complaining ruined her day.

"Hey, sorry Margie, but my five-minute eggs are done."

"I'll call back in a bit," Margie said.

Before Margie could hang up, Bailey said, "Margie, I have my day planned—I really need to accomplish some things around here. I'll see you at work tomorrow." She hung up her phone and removed her eggs from the boiling water immediately.

Bailey couldn't avoid Margie's griping at work, but she refused to let her ruin this day off. She couldn't afford to lose her hum when she'd just found it again.

She enjoyed her breakfast while leaning over the counter. After rinsing the dishes, she put a load of clothes in the washer and returned to the kitchen and emptied the dishwasher. She pulled out the vacuum cleaner and spent fifteen minutes vacuuming so that what she'd told Margie wouldn't be a lie. Plus, she loved a clean floor.

Bailey longed for a clear-conscience, hum-at-will day. She needed it before returning to work tomorrow. Work stresses had begun to affect her health.

Bailey grabbed a cup of coffee, turned on the TV, and made herself comfortable in her favorite chair. When pangs of guilt washed over her, she reminded herself that she needed this break. Doctor Hermann prescribed more quiet days for her just last week. He told her if she didn't include more relaxation in her schedule, her health issues might not improve.

Today she planned to binge-watch episodes of a show she'd considered checking out for several years. She'd seen the trailers multiple times and couldn't wait.

In between episodes, she'd read a chapter or two of a book she started a few days ago. For lunch, she would order in.

But first, she set her phone to silent mode and tossed it across the room onto the sofa. Now she couldn't reach it from where she sat without getting up. That suited her plan perfectly.

The Playlist

Her Ron would never witness this new day. Marcia found herself fixated on the thought. Her red tulips bloomed, the buds on the maple trees plumped, and a robin hopped on their front lawn while she focused on how sad it was that Ron would miss these sights of spring this year.

What a difference a missed red light can make. According to the newspaper, the young man had left home after an argument with his new wife. In his anger, his old pick-up truck transformed into a five-thousand-pound weapon. When the truck hit Ron's car on the driver's side, the force killed Ron on impact.

The poor young man. Only twenty-two years old. Stupid boy. And his poor wife. Marcia imagined their

marriage would be hard-pressed to survive such an incident. And she thought of the boy's parents. Marcia knew
nothing about them, but she wept for them too.

Tests revealed no alcohol or drugs were present in
the young man's system. The weakness of his temper—
maybe his only vice—had been powerful enough to end
the life of her husband. Marcia knew she didn't have
the strength to mourn all of them today, so she would
focus on Ron for now. She would visit his grave. So many
people hovered around on the day of the funeral at the
gravesite. Her head spun thinking of it.

She decided to bring a folding chair and use her
phone to play some of their favorite songs. Ron loved
listening to music. This time he wouldn't hear, unless he
could listen from heaven, but at least his body would be
near. Marcia planned to listen for both of them. And she
wanted to say a proper goodbye.

In the days to follow, she planned to focus on letting
go of her anger. She wanted to forgive the young man
whose temper crushed her world. Marcia refused to
let that sort of volatile anger bind itself to her heart. It
needed to be confronted before it took a permanent hold.

Marcia knew she didn't want to become a bitter old
woman. She wanted to forgive, but first, she would visit
the cemetery and discuss everything with God and Ron.
Her favorite weather app forecasted the sort of spring
day that her husband had adored. Seventy-five degrees
and sunny.

Turquoise Parade

Like many decisions they'd battled during their twenty-two years of marriage, Jennifer and Zeph had argued about the color to paint the exterior of their home. Jennifer was beyond bored with its drab shade of brown. The house across the street from theirs was another lighter shade of a similar brown, and the two homes on either side were both an uninspiring shade of gray.

Jennifer was weary of the dullness of their house color. She was tired of her routine, tired of her plain-sounding name, tired of her job, and tired of never getting what she wanted. Everything about her life seemed ordinary and humdrum.

She resolved to make a statement with the exterior

house paint decision. The house color should make her happy, she thought. She wanted her choice to cheer her at the end of a tiresome day at her mind-numbing job.

Jennifer decided to choose one of her favorite colors—a bright shade of turquoise. After a trip to the paint store, she brought home several paint swatches. The ones that contained every shade of turquoise and teal available. She favored the most exciting hues. In the end, she selected three versions of turquoise. One of these three would definitely add a measure of excitement to their dull lives. She showed the swatches to her husband.

"No way! I thought you knew me. You know that the worst ten minutes of my life each week are when I have to make the summary presentations on Mondays. I prefer not to stick out at work, but I have no choice. I'd really prefer our house not be an attention-grabber in the neighborhood. All the other homes are painted in understated, muted tones. Can't we be a normal family rather than draw attention to ourselves? Can't we just fit in and be regular? I've stood out all my life with my height and my name. Do you know what it's like to be almost seven feet tall with a name like Zephyr? Do we have to be the weirdos on the street and draw attention to ourselves?"

"What the heck is wrong with your name? Zeph is a great name."

"Try spelling Z-e-p-h-y-r thirty times a month."

"There's no way I would have married some guy with a super common name—one as common as mine."

"Jennifer's a beautiful name," he said.

"Turquoise is a beautiful color. I have it narrowed down to Triumphant Teal, Peacock Blue, or Turquoise Parade."

"None of those sound fitting for an introvert."

Jennifer didn't like to disagree. She hated arguments, but she decided when she woke up that morning to hold her ground on the subject. Zeph had his way when they named their son Michael. He had his way when they selected a location for their last vacation. She wanted Disney World or Hawaii. She wanted someplace new and exciting. Instead, they drove to Canada to go fishing. On the way, they spent half a day at the locks, watching the boats go up and down. Thinking about it, Jennifer shook her head.

"It's my house, too, and I'd really like us to choose a color that's not mundane. One that won't put me to sleep when I drive up to it after a work day. I want a color that makes me happy."

Zeph held his hands up. "I give up. If you hire painters and make the arrangements, you can pick the color. We've already learned the hard way that neither one of us knows what we're doing with a paint brush. It's important to hire someone who'll do a professional-looking job. Be sure to check reviews. And this better not be another bicycle incident!"

"That was ten years ago!"

Jennifer had selected a bicycle. By the time they arrived home, she changed her mind about the color. They drove back and paid a 15 percent re-stocking surcharge to exchange the bike.

"Good grief. Time to let that example go!" she said. "You get your way with everything. I wanted to make something exciting for dinner, but you had to have hamburgers."

"What's wrong with hamburgers? I love a good hamburger," Zeph said.

"What's wrong with trying something different? I could have cooked the hamburger and used it to make rotini pasta with marinara sauce or manicotti or something. We've had hamburgers every Tuesday for the past ten years, and I'm sick of it. I want my way with the color of the house."

Zeph held up his hands in surrender again. "Go for it, but when you don't like it, don't come to me. Houses are too expensive to re-do when you don't like the color."

The painters arrived at seven o'clock as Jennifer was leaving for work. They told her the job would take several days, but they'd try to have most of the front done by the time she made it home from work.

When Zeph arrived home, he found Jennifer lying on the bed crying. He sat on his side of the bed and asked her what was wrong.

"Were your eyes closed as you drove up to the house? On the miniature paint swatch, the color looked beautiful, but it doesn't work for the exterior of a home. And now I have to look at it for the next ten or twenty years. I hate to say it, but you may have been right." Jennifer put her face down on her pillow, and her shoulders shook with her sobs.

"Get the paint lady on the phone. Keep calling or emailing her until she responds. Tell her we're changing our minds about the color. Let's head to the store together and find a shade of blue or green you like, but then we'll look at it on one of their brochures that display house fronts. Or we'll hunt online for other homes painted that exact color to make sure we like the look of it. Maybe someone at the paint store can help us."

Jennifer rolled over to her side and grabbed a tissue from her nightstand. She sat up and blew her nose.

"Tell the lady you'll send the name of our new color choice to her tonight. Tomorrow maybe they can work on the white trim or the front door or something. Maybe one of them can pick up the new paint color if we order it tonight."

Zeph walked around the bed and pulled Jennifer to a standing position. She wiped her nose again, then tilted her head back and looked up more than a foot to see Zeph's face. She couldn't bring herself to say thank you. Apologizing wasn't her style either. But she did smile and give her husband a hug.

He hugged her back and kissed the top of her head. "Let's go, shorty." He nudged her toward the doorway. "On the way home, we'll pick up dinner at the fast-food restaurant of your choice. It doesn't even need to be a hamburger place. Yep! You've married an exciting man. You never know for sure what you're going to get, even on a Tuesday night."

Talk of the Pushkin

J ane placed a finger on her lips and shook her head slowly from side to side before speaking to Carmen.

"Can you believe Isabella?" Jane said. Sitting with perfect posture as always, she took a soundless sip of her hot cinnamon tea. "When I mentioned our visit to the Pushkin, she didn't even know what I was talking about. No clue. Imagine not knowing the Pushkin. I dreamed of going there for years. Jerry and I spent the best hours of our summer at the Pushkin last year. I cannot wait to go back. Seeing The Red Vineyard in person was heaven. Can you imagine?"

Jerry and Jane had saved for five years to make the trip of her dreams to the Pushkin come true, but Jane kept that secret to herself. Jerry kept warning her it was a once-in-a-lifetime trip, but she hoped he was wrong.

Carmen had no idea what the Pushkin was, but she nodded. She'd be sure to look it up when she reached the parking lot.

"I know what you mean," Carmen said. "I mentioned my new 5 Series to her, and Isabella was clueless."

Jane chuckled as she took her phone out of her purse. Pretending to send a quick text, she made a note to remind herself to look up *5 Series*. It sounded like a vehicle, but she wasn't sure. She planned to search the term as soon as she was home.

Driving Home from the Hospital

I f Dee could stay awake long enough to make it home, there might be eggs in the fridge. Maybe. She would boil a couple, shower, and go to bed. Dee remembered reading about a man who survived over thirty years on bread and water alone. She could freeze bread. *I'll stock up on some as soon as possible.* What she didn't have was time or energy to mess with meals.

Dee noticed a pickup accelerating behind her when she checked her rearview mirror. The truck drew almost close enough to touch her rear bumper.

She glanced at her speedometer and engaged her cruise control.

I don't dare go much faster than fifty-five, she thought. *There is no way I can afford a ticket.* The hospital bills were far beyond what they could handle already. A speeding ticket might land them in the poorhouse. The pickup driver would get a lesson in patience tonight—whether he wanted one or not.

The driver honked his horn. Dee accelerated her cruise control to four miles over the speed limit. Her friend was ticketed at five miles over not long ago, but she'd never heard of four miles over causing trouble.

He honked his horn again. This time, he held it down—for effect, Dee supposed. She felt tears on her cheeks. Two more miles. The oncoming traffic didn't look as if it would let up to allow him to pass. Even at this late hour. If only she could find a convenient spot to pull over.

Dee reached her turn at last. The truck accelerated, and with a final lengthy honk of his horn, he somehow missed scraping her rear bumper as he pulled from behind her and squealed past. Loosening her grip on her now-sweaty steering wheel, she held one hand up in front of her face to confirm the shaking. No surprise there.

Driving under the speed limit now and reminding herself to breathe deep breaths in and out as she went, she continued the last two blocks down her quiet street. *A deep breath through your nose. Exhale through your mouth*, she coached herself.

No other cars were on the road here. Front lights at almost every home on their street were out for the night. The sight calmed her. She loved their neighborhood.

As she stepped from the garage to the back porch, the light detected her motion as if to welcome her home. Right before his hospitalization a few weeks ago, her husband had installed the new light. She smiled for a moment as she remembered the day.

Forget the man in the truck, she told herself. Forget the hospital bills. Two eggs and bed. That's it.

As she stood under the porch light while digging in her handbag for the key, she noticed a brown paper sack a few feet to the right, leaning against the house. She bent down to peek inside and picked it up by its handles.

After turning on the kitchen light, she set the bag on the table and removed her jacket, but not before double-checking she'd locked the door behind her. A clear zippered pouch perched on top revealed chocolate chip cookies. She took one out and inhaled slowly. It smelled delicious. She snuck a bite and then another. The note taped to the side of the bag read:

Dee,

We've been thinking of you and hoped a few groceries might help. I made beef stew for the family tonight and have included two small containers you can either refrigerate or freeze. Also, we guessed you might be able to use a quart of milk, a dozen eggs, some bread, and coffee. My daughter baked cookies today, so we've included

*several of those, too. Our Michael will tend
to your grass until your husband is back home
where he belongs. We are praying. Much love to
you and Kevin!*

Your neighbor,

Renee

Dee opened the fridge to put the eggs away on the empty shelf. It didn't even register that she'd been out of eggs. Beef stew for a late dinner tonight sounded perfect. The second serving went into the fridge. She'd eat it tomorrow or the next night. Dee decided to freeze half the bread after she pulled a slice from the package to go with her beef stew. She would not give the pickup driver another thought. Not if she could help it.

Milk Money

W hat are we doing this afternoon, Mom?" Brie asked.

Six months earlier, Andrea had officially designated Saturdays as Larson family time. They attacked cleaning and laundry on Saturday mornings. The girls worked hard alongside their mother to get their home picked up, vacuumed, and dusted. Family fun time commenced right before lunch.

"It's two days before payday. We have no money to do anything," Andrea said. "We'll need to eat lunch at home today. You can choose between egg salad and peanut butter sandwiches, and we can have applesauce. Whatever we plan, it'll have to be free. We could watch a movie together here, play some board games, or drive over to the park on Atwood Avenue and walk around. The gardens are beautiful this time of year, and I have plenty of gas in the tank. What do you girls think?"

"Why can't we start a fund and set aside something each week in a savings account, Mom? Then we'd have money for Saturday afternoon adventures like going to the rink or the theater or the amusement park. I wish we could do something special once in a while," said Brie, Andrea's eleven-year-old daughter.

"Saving is a fine idea. We used to have a savings account, but it's dried up since Dad passed. It always seems there's not enough income to set aside for savings. I'm thankful I have a good job now, but with bills to pay, it can be hard to save."

"My teacher Mr. Beckman says it's simple to save. Just deposit ten or twenty percent of your wages as soon as you're paid, before you even touch your money," Brie said.

"Good for Mr. Beckman, dear, but sometimes it's easier to talk about saving money than to do it. I'll bet your teacher gets paid every week or every other week, and I'm sure he makes more than I do. I miss the days of being paid every Friday. I used to love that. So much. There's nothing like a paycheck in your hand at the end of a week, and an entire weekend off with cash in hand. Those were the days. Before you girls were born, your daddy and I both used to get paid on Fridays. Just imagine."

Andrea gave the kitchen counter a final swipe. "We have to face the fact that we've gone from two paychecks in our household down to one. Getting paid only once a month seems to make it even harder for me to budget everything too. The last couple of days of each month can be tough. We can do it, though. Only two more days left. Monday is payday."

"I hate to mention it, Mom," Claire said, "but we're out of milk. What are we going to do for breakfast tomorrow? We used the last of it this morning." Claire's lower lip trembled.

Andrea noticed and tried to keep things upbeat.

"Oh, shoot. That's right. Well, at least we have plenty of cereal. There are still two unopened boxes. We're rich as rich can be. We'll just have to do one of our roundups to hunt down enough for milk money." She wagged her finger at the girls. "But no other spending until payday. Nothing else for two more days." She held up two fingers and smiled at the same time. "We can do it. We have soup, bread, cereal, applesauce, carrots, and bananas. We'll be just fine."

"Can't we just use your credit card for milk, Mom?"

"I would love to, Brie, but it's maxed out." Andrea shrugged her shoulders.

"Roundup time. I'll check the bottom of my purse for coins. Brie, you get the quarters out of the coin tray in the car. Claire, you check the junk drawer. Whenever I find coins lying around, I toss them into the junk drawer."

"We know, Mom." The girls responded in unison. Of course, they knew. This was not their first roundup. This scavenging for food money happened often enough that they knew the drill.

"I'll check my coat pockets. If we're lucky we'll scrounge up enough for a quart, or maybe even a half gallon. Every once in a while, I think ahead and leave a dollar or two in one of my jacket pockets in anticipation of a day like this."

"We know, Mom!"

"Cross your fingers, kids."

Andrea opened the front closet and began to check each of the coat pockets. She held an empty plastic bag in one hand, and as she searched pockets, she tossed any receipts, wrappers, and tissues she came across. In her grey zippered sweatshirt, she found a crumpled dollar bill. "I found a dollar!" Andrea liked to call out her progress to make a game of it.

As she was checking the jacket furthest back to the left in the closet, she noticed her old spring coat lying on the floor in the back corner. She picked it up and discovered a twenty-dollar bill in the side pocket.

No, wait.

She checked the other pocket and found one in the other side too. She couldn't believe it. Andrea was never that generous with herself when she left money behind in her pockets. She had no memory of sticking that much cash there. After thinking for a moment or two, she realized it couldn't have been her. She had never hidden a twenty-dollar bill before. Not even a ten. It couldn't have been her.

"Girls, come here. Hurry. Look what I found in my old spring jacket pocket! Can you believe it?"

Andrea held out the two twenty-dollar bills and the crumpled one-dollar bill. "Over forty dollars! We need to celebrate. Let's get ready to go as soon as we've eaten our sandwiches. How about we take a walk around the gardens and then play a few board games. We'll pick up milk on the way home from the gardens. Then, to celebrate, why don't we splurge tonight and try the taco drive-through place for dinner?"

"I'd rather have a burger," Claire said. "Do you think we could afford three burgers?"

"Claire, I'm so happy about finding this money, I'll go through the taco drive-through and then the burger drive-through just for you." Andrea rarely consented to eating out or getting fast food, believing it was less expensive to eat at home.

"I'd never leave twenty dollars in my pocket on purpose. Or forty. I keep thinking someone else must have done it, but I can't imagine who it might have been."

LORI LIPSKY

"You had that coat when Dad was here, but I don't remember you wearing it since Dad died," Brie said. "Dad knew how crazy you get hunting for money before payday. Do you think he left it back there in the corner for you to find on a day like today?"

"Maybe so. Maybe it was hanging up on the end of the rod and then it fell to the floor," Andrea said. "I'd have found the money sooner if the coat had been hanging up. That closet gets so messy."

Andrea pulled a notepad and pen out of the junk drawer clutter and made a short list.

"You know what I think, girls? Your dad loved us, and I think this is one of those reminders from heaven to help us keep going. After a gallon of milk, tacos, and a burger, let's use the rest to open a savings account."

Andrea waved one of the twenties in the air. "I wonder if the credit union will allow an account with only a twenty-dollar balance? We can call it our Saturday adventure account. If we drink water at home for dinner tonight instead of getting soda at the drive-through, we'll probably have twenty dollars left over to open an account. And that's before payday and everything."

Andrea continued. "Just think, girls. We'll be rich." She did a little dance and started to chuckle. The girls soon joined in, and the three of them enjoyed a good laugh together before heading out on their Saturday adventure.

Poor Oscar

When she moved in on Saturday, Penny positioned her office desk to allow her a view out the window. Her new neighborhood is an active one. Every few minutes, a neighbor passes by walking a dog on a leash. It seems everyone owns a dog, but that can't be true. Maybe only dog owners make the effort to walk around the neighborhood on wintry days.

From the side office window of her corner lot home, she views the back door of the charcoal gray house behind hers. Her new neighbor, whom she hasn't met, lets a fluffy white dog out the back door. Penny names the dog Oscar until more accurate information comes to light. He sniffs around happily for five minutes after first doing his required business.

An attractive four-foot cedar wood fence borders the entire backyard of the gray house neighbors. The slight elevation of her lot allows Penny a clear view of the neighbor's property, even with the fence. She notices that Oscar stays away from the lot line. He keeps near his home and glances at the door every few seconds.

Now, Oscar stands on the stoop, his nose to the door, tail wagging. Penny wishes she could open the door for Oscar. He looks cold and eager to be allowed back inside.

Penny takes a bathroom break and refills her coffee mug before returning to her desk. Oscar still waits. Poor Oscar. His paws must be cold on a day like this.

Should she walk over and knock on their front door? But she's the new neighbor and doesn't know Oscar's people. Penny hopes for kind souls she can live next door to in peace and safety. She checks the temperature, and when she sees it registers not much below the freezing point, she relaxes a bit.

"Step on the mat," she says. "Step on the mat, Oscar. It might help your little paws." He steps on the thick jute mat and seems to find comfort there. Penny knows he doesn't want to block the door in case it opens, so he paces back and forth, nose to the door.

Penny yells. But no one hears. Not even Oscar.

"Bark, Oscar. Bark!"

She unlocks her window, looks both ways, and yells once again for the dog to bark. Oscar doesn't respond.

Penny barks. Oscar still doesn't respond. He paces. She notices his tail no longer wags.

Penny knows her friend Sheila would have been over there by now, pounding on the door, scolding the people to take better care of their precious dog. Penny can't help being more reserved and cautious. After all, she may still live next to these people ten years from now. Ten years is a long time—she decides she should proceed with caution. Since Oscar wears a good coat of fur, she decides against the aggressive Sheila-like approach.

A long-time client has a call scheduled with Penny. She receives the call and knows she won't need her computer for the next ten or fifteen minutes. This particular client likes to chat about personal matters and tends to enjoy lengthy conversations.

Thinking that a watched pot never boils, she stands up and paces the living room and kitchen area as she listens. Penny gets more steps in for the day and avoids the two windows in her home that face the gray house.

By the time her long-winded client finishes and says goodbye, she's resolved to put on her coat and gloves and walk over to meet the neighbors.

She steps cautiously into her office and peers out the window in search of the fluffy white dog but doesn't catch sight of Oscar. Yesterday's snowfall covers the ground with a clean blanket of white, so she takes extra time to be sure Oscar is no longer outside.

She exhales the big breath she didn't realize she was holding.

At the end of her workday, Penny spends a half hour rearranging the extra bedroom she's converted to an office for her work-from-home job. She moves her desk so it faces the other window. This gives her a new view—now she'll look out the front of her house toward the red brick home across the street. She wishes Oscar well, but until further notice, she closes the blinds overlooking the charcoal gray house with the cedar fence.

The Handbell Professor

Before the end of the first week, we grew fond of our conductor, Professor Pearson. Students spoke well of the course and its instructor during breaks and after class. The graduate-level handbell course involved two weeks of daily six-hour rehearsals. At the end of week two, the class would culminate in two performances of a well-advertised concert.

A large private school in my home state had hired me two months earlier to head its small team of music instructors. The position began with the fall semester. The principal advised me to take the advanced handbell course. The class fulfilled the state mandate to keep my degree updated, and I would earn three graduate-level credits, which would help bump me to the next tier on the pay scale.

Part of my new position involved directing three hand-bell choirs. The church that sponsored the school owned the expensive handbell set. The principal loved handbell choirs and resolved that our school would use them as a music education tool. She decided handbells would make an appearance at our Christmas concert as well.

Classes were held in Milwaukee, two hours from my home, so I rented a room at a residential hotel just six blocks from the course location. Each day when class ended, I stopped to pick up dinner from a local restaurant and then spent two or three hours in the evening studying and marking my music.

For each musical selection, I'd been assigned the F and G bells above middle C and all adjacent sharps and flats. Most performers in an average handbell choir play one or two bells, but this graduate-level handbell course required more. The advanced arrangements contained plenty of runs and key changes. Sometimes I needed to assist my classmates with nearby bells, and sometimes they helped me.

During some of the pieces, I handled six or seven bells. Knowing when to pick them up, when to switch bells, and which hand to use was a challenge. My music needed to be well-marked so I wouldn't miss an entrance or any of my assigned notes.

In the middle of the second week of class, someone mentioned that the director's birthday was on Friday. One of the students purchased a cake and brought it in to celebrate. She brought candles too. Word passed table by table that at two-thirty, when someone started singing "Happy Birthday," we should all join in.

Professor Pearson teared up and wiped his nose as we sang. The tall, grey-haired man didn't seem like the type to cry over a cake and a song. The woman who brought the cake announced we should all join the group in the nearby kitchen for birthday celebration refreshments. Ninety minutes of class remained, so nobody left the building.

We gathered two-deep around a long table in the kitchen area. The woman who brought the cake, plates, and napkins lit the candles, and Professor Pearson blew them out. Someone called out the word *speech*, so we all joined along, saying, "speech, speech."

The woman used a kitchen knife to cut into the cake. She handed the first piece—a large one—to the man of honor, and she said, "The rest of you will have your piece after Professor Pearson gives a short speech." She worked on cutting the cake while he spoke.

"I'm seventy years old today." Professor Pearson commanded our attention without much effort. After working under his direction for ten long days, we all adored him. At least those who sat near me during the class did. No one looked surprised when he shared his age, and no one interrupted.

"This means more than you know," he said. "It's the first time in my life I've ever had a birthday cake. It's the first time anyone has sung the birthday song for me, and the first time I've blown out birthday candles."

I wondered how that was possible but realized I really knew very little about the professor.

The woman led us in a round of applause. I recognized her—she sat at the long table behind me and handled some of the larger bells. She wore wrist supports all week—I'd been thankful I didn't have to ring those big bells. The heavy bells can be a challenge for people who lack strong wrists.

The large sheet cake was big enough to serve everyone in the class, and the professor was able to take the remainder home with him. After hearing that he'd never had a birthday cake before, I assumed he was a single man. He didn't wear a wedding ring, but I didn't know for sure.

That evening, before the concert, I couldn't stop thinking about the professor's words. I wondered how in the world he made it to seventy years old without ever having a birthday cake. As we waited to file onto the stage, I thanked the woman who brought the cake, and I introduced myself.

"How did you know it was his birthday?" I asked.

"He doesn't have much of a presence on social media, but I did find a few bios and noticed his birth date.

I thought a little birthday celebration would be a nice surprise for him."

"I assumed he was a personal friend or that you'd worked with him in the past."

"No. I just think he's a wonderful director. He doesn't know my name, but maybe I'll introduce myself after our concert. I thought a cake would be a nice surprise. The store delivered it so I didn't need to carry it in. My wrists can only take so much." She held her wrapped wrists up in front of her face.

"Those lower bells are something else. You're doing a great job," I said. "Thanks for the cake today. I'd love to chip in if I can." I handed her a folded bill, and to my surprise, she accepted it and put it in her pocket.

"You know, over two dozen of us took this class and ate the cake, but you're the only one besides the professor who thanked me or offered to share in the cost. One woman did help clean up the kitchen today after our little party. I really appreciate your offer to help defray the cost."

At that moment, Professor Pearson walked past and beckoned those at the front of the line to follow him onto the stage. As soon as the professor stepped into view, the audience applauded. We followed him single file and took our places behind the appropriate bells. I squinted my eyes, and beyond the bright lights, I could see the seats of the auditorium were filled to capacity.

Our conductor stepped onto the podium, looking handsome in his performance tuxedo. Professor Pearson raised his baton, and the handbell concert commenced.

An Unwanted Commencement

On her fiftieth birthday, despite her fierce efforts and those of her husband and their medical practitioners, Rhonda found herself childless. By the time she turned sixty, Rhonda could add widowed to her state of affairs. Her husband breathed his last only two months before her sixtieth birthday, following a long illness. Rhonda was left behind, weary, and worn out.

Thankfully, I wasn't left penniless, she kept thinking. If it'd been left to her, she'd have put off saving for retirement until the year before retirement. She tried to remember to thank God every morning that James had been level-headed and budget-conscious enough for the two of them.

How they'd fought over money the first few years of marriage. She cringed to think of it. Now she was reaping the benefits of her husband's financial prudence. Before he died, they owned their home, two cars, and a vacation condo in Florida. The couple had no debt and plenty of savings. Because of James, she would not have to worry about money, unlike so many other widows she'd heard of.

Rhonda could continue at her current standard of living for the rest of her life, even if she lived to the age of one hundred or beyond. But for now, she was so exhausted she had no interest in living or otherwise. Once arrangements were finalized and the funeral and burial took place, Rhonda saw her doctor. Following his advice, she took to her bed and tried to rest.

Several days later, when food had run out, she went online and discovered for the first time that she could pay a driver to pick food up for her and deliver it to her front door. Paying online meant she wouldn't need to answer the door in her robe. She posted a sign next to the doorbell instructing drivers to leave food deliveries on the front porch. Several of her favorite restaurants also delivered, so that helped her through the next few weeks.

On the evening after her birthday, Rhonda dressed and headed to the grocery store to stock up. She chose Thursday evening at eight o'clock on purpose so she'd be unlikely to run into anyone she knew.

How strange it seemed to walk into the grocery store. Somehow, life rolled on as always. As other shoppers went about their business, she moved inside a hazy bubble, reaching for her husband's favorite chips and the rump roast he loved, then drawing back her hand. She discovered her change in marital status even altered a task as simple as grocery shopping.

Trying to decide what to buy, it dawned on her that although she'd given up fish because of her husband's allergy, she no longer needed to do so. She added a piece of fresh wild-caught salmon to her basket. To pick up tuna for sandwiches like her mother used to make, she steered her cart back to the canned fish aisle. She hadn't made tuna sandwiches since her single days.

She grabbed several cans of salmon also since she had no interest in coming to the store on a daily basis to purchase fresh fish. She used to love salmon patties, until the allergy of the man she loved put that to an end.

Guilt tugged at her. She'd much rather have her husband back than eat the best fish in the world. *Fish is okay,* she told herself. *He'd be fine with you eating fish. He isn't coming back. It's okay if you find pleasure in eating fish. It's okay.*

Rhonda picked up a small tray of prepared fruit. Again, it dawned on her she could choose her favorites now. She hadn't purchased raspberries or blackberries in years. She placed a pint of each in her cart.

Rhonda reflected on the compromises made in a marriage. She envisioned her husband's shopping cart if he were left behind without her. She doubted he would agonize over the selections like she was doing. Men didn't wrestle over things like that, she guessed.

The struggle continued in the milk aisle. Her husband had preferred one percent. She brazenly grabbed a half gallon of the two percent she'd been raised on. Emotional challenges struck in every aisle.

Her plan of avoiding friends and acquaintances worked out, but she arrived home, unloaded a month's worth of groceries, and realized she'd missed the experience of running into people she knew. She started to cry but stopped herself. She missed her work friends, having taken an open-ended leave of absence. She missed her quilting club and her book club friends. She missed her tennis league.

Avoiding others and being alone every day had been fine for a while, but being all by herself was getting old. Maybe it was time to mingle with the living again.

Rhonda doubted she'd ever adjust to unloading the groceries and putting them away by herself. James possessed a number of fine qualities, but always carrying the luggage and the groceries for her had been one of his finest.

Once the groceries were put away, Rhonda sat down with a notebook and made a list of five friends she liked best in the world. Friends who lived nearby. She set a modest goal for herself—one she knew she could handle.

Before a month passed, she would call each of the women on the list. She'd invite them, one at a time, out for dinner, out for coffee, or to a movie.

She wouldn't put life off for another moment. She'd attack her list and call the first person before another hour of life passed. Colleen had shown herself to be a loyal friend throughout the ordeal. Rhonda grabbed her phone and called Colleen.

The Metal Comb

B rooke's host family and friends scoffed at her concerns about lice. They didn't understand her obsession. So prevalent was the issue in the area where she stayed, there was no escaping it.

A community art gallery in the Philippines had selected to host Brooke as their area artist in residence. During the three months allowed by her work visa, she was provided an assistant to translate and help with transportation while she worked on a socially poignant photography project.

Brooke bought a lice comb and the only brand of lice shampoo available in the area. Everyone said the shampoo wouldn't work. They told her the local lice had developed immunity against it. Brooke tried anyway, without success. The bamboo nit comb she purchased fell apart when she tried to use it. She bought a second comb, and the same thing happened. Metal combs were unavailable, and bamboo ones weren't strong enough.

Brooke's host, a single mother, had purchased a two-bedroom home with a large living room. She converted the family gathering space into an art gallery. Brooke and her designated assistant slept in one of the bedrooms. Each were provided a twin bed. Everyone else in the house slept in the second bedroom: the host, her children, her sister, her brother-in-law, and their children—there were five children in all. Brooke never looked into the other bedroom.

She had no idea how they made it work.

During the day, the younger kids felt free to hop on Brooke's bed and lay their heads on her pillow. Even if the shampoo and comb worked, she would've been reinfected.

Brooke and the other adults and their extended family supported Perlita, a local artist, whenever she sang at nearby venues and bars. More than once, Perlita said to Brooke, "Lice are no big deal. Just have your auntie pick out the nits."

Other friends said, "Have your auntie get the lice out." But Brooke had no mother or auntie in the country. She didn't learn until later that the word auntie could mean friend, but she didn't have any friends there anyway.

Brooke did her best to keep her distance from others and didn't let herself touch anyone. When her visa expired, she took the opportunity to visit Perth, Australia, for two weeks before returning to North America. In Perth, she met an older woman in the hostel where she stayed. The two got along well.

One day they were sitting on a bench talking, and the woman laid her head on Brooke's shoulder in a friendly gesture. Brooke stood up quickly. She didn't want to confess to the lice problem, but she hoped the woman wasn't offended by her sudden movement.

When Brooke arrived back home in the states, she immediately showered with the lice shampoo her mother had purchased for her. She spent an hour or so in the bathroom working through her hair with a metal lice comb. Then her mother took over to help with the back of Brooke's head. Brooke showed her what to look for and how to do it. Her mother spent time going through her hair until all the nits were gone.

Brooke ate a casual dinner with her family. Exhausted, she climbed into her own bed for the first time in months. Her mother had washed the bedding, and even ironed her pillowcase. Everything felt clean and fresh. She fell asleep in less than five minutes. For the first time in a long while, Brooke slept the entire night without waking once.

Planting Annuals

Josie knelt to dig in the flowerbed with her new trowel. She'd dreamed of having her own flower garden for years, and here it was. Her husband devoted hours the day before, removing sod and turning soil by hand with their new spade. Now that the soil was prepared, she planned to plant the first flowers on their new property. She carried out the first tray of blooms from the garage.

She and her husband were thrilled to be settling into their single-family home. After living on the fourth floor of an apartment building for their first six years of marriage, Josie's dream had been to have a lawn large enough to fit a small flowerbed. If they could not find a house with a lawn, she hoped for a patio or balcony to display potted flowers.

Their real estate agent somehow managed to find the young couple a home in their price range with all three—a lawn, a balcony, and a patio.

"This is as close to paradise as I'm going to get here on earth," Josie said as she entered their home with Nate for the first time after the closing.

Nate's top wish list items were met as well. The couple's agent negotiated a price fifteen thousand dollars under the asking cost, the home was move-in ready, and his wife was ecstatic.

Josie couldn't wait to meet her new neighbors. She decided that gardening in the front yard would be a great way to meet and interact with neighbors as they walked by. Their new home even had a front porch. Once her planting was completed, she could rest on the porch and enjoy the results of her labor.

As a housewarming gift, the previous neighbor left behind two old Adirondack chairs. Josie planned to paint them white. They would do for the next few years until she could talk Nate into buying new ones.

Josie hadn't put a single flower in the ground when the neighbor from across the street stopped over. Josie stood up. She brushed off her hands and the knees of her jeans. The neighbor introduced herself as Rita Hadley and welcomed Josie to the neighborhood.

"I see you're planting annuals. I'm not sure begonias will do well on this side of the house. You might want to try the backyard. Janice has that empty bed in the backyard, you know." Rita took a second to breathe and continued right on. "I've found it's much more cost-effective to plant perennials, though. Are you sure you want to put money into begonias, petunias, and impatiens? It might be a wiser investment to plant perennials. Every time you spend a dollar, you're casting a vote for the kind of world we live in, you know."

Josie wanted to say she'd been planning on annuals since before they purchased the house. She'd measured, plotted, and purchased more than half the flowers. She wanted to tell Rita she used to help her grandma with planting every spring, and now that her grandma was gone, she wanted to continue the tradition with the same annuals they always planted together.

But Josie she didn't say anything. Before she mustered the courage to respond, Rita mentioned she had a full day of errands planned. She left as quickly as she had arrived. Josie went into her house and cried.

That evening she spoke with Nate about what had happened.

Nate said, "We saved a long time to buy this house. We signed the papers. We're going to be paying the bank a boatload of money every month for the next fifteen years. Janice may be a nice lady, but she doesn't own this house anymore. I wish her well in her new place, but this is our house now. It's our home. It's not Janice's. If you want annuals, we're going to have as many annuals as you want. You've been talking about a flower garden since the day we met. I know how important it is to you."

"I hate to admit this, but Rita may have a point." Josie used to like the name Rita, but it was quickly losing its popularity in her mind. "Perennials are more expensive initially, but if a gardener does it right, they'll last multiple seasons."

"Josie, you've been talking about annuals forever. I'm not even sure what annuals are, but you are going to have your annuals. Go wild. Tomorrow we'll be home all day. While I'm cutting the grass, do more planting if you want. If the neighbor comes over again, I'll stop the mower and have a chat with her."

Josie couldn't believe the words coming out of her frugal husband's mouth. Nate never said words like "go wild" in regard to spending. He didn't use those types of phrases. The neighbor must have rubbed him the wrong way too. Josie didn't understand why Nate was so riled up, but she had no intention of arguing against funds for her garden plans.

The next day after church, Josie finished planting the flowers she'd purchased. She planned to shop for more later that afternoon, so she went inside to clean up. While Nate was finishing mowing, Rita walked over to introduce herself to him. Only one strip of grass remained before he finished the job, but out of courtesy, he stopped the motor.

"I see your wife planted a lot of annuals. I tried to tell her they might not do well, but I see she went ahead anyway."

"Josie wanted to try them. She's been planning her flower garden for years."

"It seems a waste of money to plant flowers where they might not do well. Janice has that bed in back. The shade might be better there."

"True, but neighbors can't see the flower patch if it's in our backyard."

"You may not have noticed but most of the neighbors use reel mowers," Rita said. "You know, the kind without an engine. It keeps the neighborhood noise down and saves fuel. It's healthier for all of us if you switch. Every time you spend money, you're casting a vote for the kind of world we live in. Have you noticed that? I think it's true."

Nate adored his new self-propelled push mower. "I just bought the mower last week, and it's used now, so I think we're stuck for the next few years. Those hand mowers seem like they might be challenging to use if the grass gets long, or when the ground is hilly. We have a steep incline in the backyard, you know."

"I do hope you don't plan to let your lawn grow long. Where did you get the mower? If you bought it at Harry's here in town, he'll take it back for a full refund. Just tell him Rita sent you."

Nate had indeed bought the mower at Harry's, but he had no intention of returning it. He said nothing.

While Josie weeded her begonia bed later that month, Rita strolled over. "I noticed your bed needed weeding the other day. It would be a shame to spend such a fortune on flowers only to lose them to weeds."

Josie's face felt warm. She knew she probably looked bright red. "The mosquitoes have been horrible, especially with all the rain we've had. The ground was pretty soft too. Today is much better with the breeze."

"I thought mosquitoes might be the trouble. I have just the thing for you." Rita pulled out a glass bottle filled with yellow liquid. She shook it near Josie's face. "I make this concoction every year. All the neighbors love it. Mosquitoes detest it. You'll never have to put your weeding off again."

Rita held the bottle out and placed it in Josie's hand. "It's pesticide free and perfectly safe. Don't spend money on bug spray loaded with harmful chemicals. This bottle sells for $9.50. Only $9.50 and you'll never have to let your weeds go again."

"I'm sorry, I don't have any money on me," Josie said. The last thing she wanted to do was give the woman money.

"That's okay. I'm not in a hurry. I'll wait while you go inside and get it."

Josie reluctantly stood up, brushed off, and went in the house. She brought out a ten-dollar bill. "I don't have change. You can just keep it." She kneeled and continued with her weeding.

"I hope you'll use it," said Rita. She placed the bottle on the front walk near Josie. "Pesticides are what's wrong with the world. Every time you spend a dollar, you're casting a vote for the kind of world we live in."

Josie took a deep breath and gathered her courage. She'd prepared for this moment. She even practiced with Nate and her mother.

"What a thought-provoking phrase. In fact, Nate and I have given thought to the kind of world we want to live in and how we want to spend our money," Josie said. "We've decided to invest a portion of our savings into building a fence around our little yard. We'll fit right in here with a fence. I see your neighbors on both sides have them. We're going to cast a vote for a world of privacy, respect, and independence."

Josie stood up, brushed off her pants, and walked toward the house, leaving her trowel, her gloves, and the mosquito-killing concoction from Rita on the walk next to her wave petunias. Once inside the house, Josie noticed her hands trembling. She shook her arms and hands. Then she crept down her hallway as if someone could hear, and she peeked at the front yard from behind a bedroom curtain. Josie witnessed Rita bending over her flowerbed to pull the weeds Josie had missed.

Job Security

Selena lacks the energy and ability to investigate things on her own. She likes her job. She knows the pain of being unhappy with a job, and even worse, the anguish of being out of work. She plans to continue with her position until she has a major reason to leave.

The turnover at her workplace puzzles her. Of the forty employees, she's been there the longest, and it's only been seven years for her. That's not counting old Mr. Johnson, who started on day one twenty years ago with cleaning the place and fixing things that break.

Company management requires all employees take the days between Christmas and New Year's as vacation days. *That doesn't seem right to only give your employees two weeks off per year and require them to take one of the weeks after Christmas,* she thinks. Selena doesn't care much for travel, so she won't quit for that reason. She has heard multiple complaints about the vacation policy while passing others on the way to the restroom, though.

When she returned to her office on January second this year, eight of her co-workers did not. She has no idea why. Did they quit, or were they let go? *Do they all know something I don't know?*

She's heard the younger generation doesn't keep jobs as long these days. Maybe that's the reason. The employee turnover baffles her. Most of the employees are much younger than Selena. They're in their twenties and thirties, and she's almost fifty.

Selena doesn't have access to personal information for those who left, so she can't contact them and ask. And she isn't sure it's her business anyway.

Her parents worked hard and struggled with finances their entire lives. They often advised her not to make friends in the workplace. "Just keep your head to the grindstone and give your best while you're there," they had told her. "The problem with work friends is that they begin to grumble and complain to each other, and pretty soon the complaints escalate. The griping usually makes things worse than the initial situation."

"Find your friends outside of work and save them for the weekend," they had always said.

Selena's best friend lives next door to her, and she has plenty of friends from church too.

Her dad worked forty-two years for the local telephone company. The pay wasn't great, but he had medical and dental coverage and worked hard to keep his job. He knew if he left, there'd be a line of people happy to replace him—happy to have the steady paycheck and the medical insurance. He and most other workers in the country knew jobs were scarce. They were employed at will and could be terminated at any time for any reason.

Going another generation back, her grandparents lived during the depression. She'd heard the stories her entire life. Some months they only had food because her grandpa hunted, and he and his wife gardened. Back then, if they had nothing for dinner, he could grab his gun, walk two miles to the slough, lie on his back on a piece of dry land, and wait for a flock of ducks to fly overhead. He could almost always shoot one as they flew out to feed in the morning or as they returned before sunset.

Selena knows times have changed, but most of the advice from her parents over the years has been good and helpful. She's decided to be careful and keep doing the best work she knows how to do. The health insurance is decent, and she doubts she could make more money than she earns now at another company. She enjoys her work and never has to put in overtime hours. She's decided to listen to her parents' voices in her ear, keep her head down, and mind her own business.

A Good Ham Dinner

Hank lost his wife last year after sixty years of marriage. Everyone knew what a good cook Marie had been, and they sympathized with him in his sorrow. Not only did Hank lose the companionship and love of his wife, he lost the excellent meals she served each day.

Two Sundays after Marie's funeral, his neighbors the Warrens dropped off a grocery bag filled with disposable dishes containing ham, scalloped potatoes, green beans, and apple crisp. He was touched by their generosity, but he did not like ham. He never had.

About forty years into their marriage when his wife served ham for dinner, he had what his wife and children called for years afterward: his conniption fit. When the family gathered and started eating the holiday dinner Marie cooked, the two were in the midst of a mild disagreement. Something Marie said upset Hank. As he took a bite of his food, he began a discourse of the reasons he did not like ham. She had served him ham several times a year for forty years, and he never wanted to eat ham again. In his entire life, he had never liked ham, and he refused to eat it even one more time.

Marie loved ham, but she never served it to him again. After his retirement, he was always around, so Marie never enjoyed a homemade ham dinner again.

When the Warrens had dropped off the ham dinner, he wasn't sure what to do. If his wife were around, he would have let her eat the dinner. He stored the containers in the refrigerator and didn't touch them for two days. On the third day, he decided to throw the food away. But having grown up in modest circumstances, he couldn't bring himself to do it. Maybe if he waited until the food spoiled, he'd be able to dispose of it.

His mind could think of little else, so on the fourth day Hank decided to eat the ham dinner to keep a clear conscience. As he ate, he thought of his wife. The neighbor's ham and potatoes seemed on par with hers, but everyone always said what a good cook Marie was. And they were right.

The next day, Hank phoned his neighbors. He thanked them for sharing their ham dinner with him.

"Oh, I'm happy you liked it," Annette Warren said. "We just love a good ham. It's our favorite meal. Whenever we make a ham dinner from now on, we'll run a plate over."

Hank wasn't sure how to respond. His wife had always known the perfect way to handle situations like this. Instead, he asked his neighbor if she'd seen the weather forecast for tomorrow.

The Search for a Mentor

S adie finds herself in bed an hour earlier than usual but not at all tired. Last night she couldn't get comfortable because of the baby, but tonight Baby Girl lies peaceful and calm. Only a few more weeks. She can do this, she hopes.

Her husband had left around the time they found out about the baby. "Poor timing," he'd said. *Good riddance*, she decided. *This baby deserves a father who wants to be there for his wife and his child.*

He's chosen a woman at work who is also expecting his baby, so Sadie doesn't want him back. He's made his choice.

Sadie desperately longs for a mentor. She knows she needs one. Her mother would be perfect for the job, but she's no longer available. She's up in the sky somewhere, wherever heaven is.

Scientists using strong telescopes haven't reported glimpses of heaven, but Sadie knows it's there. She wonders if it could be within sight but in an alternate dimension. Like the angels, maybe heaven is close but just invisible to her eyes.

A hand-written letter arrives every couple of months from an old friend of her mother's. Sadie reads and re-reads every word. She's tried calling, but the woman's hearing loss makes it difficult to carry on a conversation. The woman advised her she might find a mentor in Elisabeth Elliot. Like her mother, missionary Elisabeth Elliot has passed to the invisible realm, but she's left a number of books behind on earth. They're stacked on Sadie's nightstand, on loan from the library.

Since Sadie won't be tired for at least an hour, she'll begin reading. If this author doesn't seem to be a suitable mentor, she'll find another. With all the books in the world, she's bound to find a fitting guide for herself and her situation.

Before she starts to read, she sits up, grabs her robe, and steps onto her second-floor balcony. Sadie peers up as if to search for her mother. The waxing gibbous moon hangs in the clear sky, but Sadie still can't glimpse heaven. By faith, she believes they're all up there somewhere: the great street of gold, the Tree of Life, the absence of sorrow, her mother, and her grandparents. They're all waiting for her, up where the clouds usually gather. Sadie hasn't been equipped with eyes to see the invisible yet, but she knows someday she'll have them.

Baby Girl kicks and brings her thoughts back to earth. The kick reminds her she's wanted here for a time. Someone helpless and vulnerable needs her. As her mother did for her, Sadie will love this baby and give her the best she can.

Sadie's eyes search at work and at church for a woman to offer counsel. Someone to call when she needs a listening ear or when the baby has a fever, and she isn't sure what to do. In the meantime, Sadie adjusts her pillows and her body again to get comfortable. Pulling the top book from the stack, she begins to read.

Rings on her Fingers

L ana noticed a change in her left hand after the long winter. The portion of her pinkie finger past the last knuckle appeared deformed. As she dreaded, her arthritis had found its way into her hands. She decided to go shopping for some pretty rings.

The crooked finger reminded her of old Mrs. Scott and her hands. Lana's family sat in the church pew behind Mrs. Scott throughout Lana's childhood. Lana remembered Mrs. Scott sitting by herself on Sundays, but according to her mother, Mrs. Scott used to attend with her husband and her teenaged son.

By the time Lana turned three years old, Mrs. Scott's husband had passed away. Her son moved to California after his high school graduation, and he never returned, as far as Lana's mom knew.

The most wrinkled face Lana ever saw belonged to Mrs. Scott. Another woman at church celebrated her one hundredth birthday, and her face wasn't even half as wrinkled. Lana once guessed that Mrs. Scott looked about eighty, but at the time, her mother told her she was at least ten years younger than that. According to Lana's mother, Carla, Mrs. Scott earned her wrinkles through her love of gardening. Carla also thought she might have smoked when she was younger, but she wasn't sure.

Mrs. Scott spoke kindly to Lana and her family each week after church. She often told Lana how much she enjoyed hearing her pretty voice sing the hymns. She said sometimes she would just listen instead of singing because she loved Lana's voice so much.

Mrs. Scott's misshapen fingers were a sight. Arthritis viciously attacked her hands. Lana sometimes leaned forward, resting on the pew in front, her chin on her hands. For some reason, her mother allowed this. She wasn't permitted to draw or whisper, but she could lay her head on her mom's shoulder or on the forward pew.

Mrs. Scott's hands fascinated Lana. Now, decades later, Lana worried her hands were on the way to suffering a similar fate.

Old Mrs. Scott wore the prettiest rings Lana ever saw. Carla guessed aloud that once her husband died, she finally had freedom to spend their money. And once her arthritis set in, maybe she wore rings to attract attention away from her twisted fingers. Lana's mom often wondered aloud how in the world Mrs. Scott was able to get any gardening done with her poor crooked fingers.

Mom said she used to wear the same old dress to church most Sundays, but after Mr. Scott passed away, she spent some time shopping. She figured Mrs. Scott started going to the beauty salon every week too. Her hair always looked nice, and it never had when Mr. Scott was alive.

Lana hadn't seen the before and after as her mother had. "Some men are like that," Carla said.

"Like what?"

"They make sure they have the newest tools, the best mower, and every modern device they need to get their work done, but they let their wives use the same pans and dishes and utensils for fifty years. If their wife does the vacuuming, the vacuum is older than Methuselah. And they never think to suggest she buy new clothes."

"Dad isn't like that, is he?"

"No, your dad is not like that."

Lana wondered if Mrs. Scott was still alive. Her parents moved from the area long ago, and she hadn't thought of Mrs. Scott in years. She searched for her obituary and found a three-paragraph summary of her life.

Lana was delighted to discover, from the dates on her obituary, that old Mrs. Scott lived as a widow for over twenty years. She had more than two decades to wear pretty rings, dress nicely, get her hair fixed, and enjoy life. Long before she passed away, she sold the farm and bought a small house in town. According to her obituary, Mrs. Scott died peacefully in her home with loved ones surrounding her.

Ten Signs of a Healthy Marriage

A magazine article on marriage caught Beth's attention at the salon one Saturday morning. Before reading the article, she was perfectly content with the state of her marriage. She imagined the same for Nick. After five minutes of reading "10 Signs of a Healthy Marriage," the foundation of her confidence was shaken to its core. While waiting for the moisturizing treatment to do its work on her hair, Beth attempted to gain her composure with deep breathing exercises. Before discovering the marriage article, she'd read one on relaxation through deep breathing.

Number two on the magazine marriage list stated that a healthy couple shows affection throughout the day. Beth and Nick worked through conflict in the early years of their marriage over this issue. The couple struggled more with it than money or anything else. Beth's family was comfortably overt in their shows of affection, but Nick had rarely seen his parents kiss or hug each other. Beth resigned herself long ago to the fact that this was not an area of strength with Nick, and she had given up trying to change him.

Number seven on the list unsettled her the most. It stated how critical words of affirmation are if a marriage has a chance to survive. And though she remembered just yesterday she'd told Nick she was proud of him, she couldn't remember the last time he expressed affirming words to her.

Yesterday she'd run into one of the receptionists at Nick's firm. Gayle let it slip how impressed she was by Nick's kindness. She said he was the nicest partner at the firm. "Everybody thinks so. We're all fond of him."

Beth valued kindness more than almost any quality and told Nick last night how proud she was of him. She had even expressed thanks to him for working hard to support them for the past ten years. Nick was a good worker, and she was proud of him for that.

In an effort to calm herself, Beth considered that Nick's parents weren't the type of people to express words of affection either, but they were good people. The two were good to her, and they were still married after more than thirty years.

LORI LIPSKY

Still, Beth was troubled about the state of her marriage. When she made it home, she went in, laid down on her bed, and stared at the ceiling. Nick found her in the bedroom after he finished the lawn.

"You're home from getting your hair done. Are you okay?"

"Yep." *He won't even say anything about my hair,* she thought. *I could color it orange, and he wouldn't even notice.*

"I'm going to take a quick shower, but when I'm done, do you want to run to the discount store together?"

The sky opened up, and rain poured down all the way to the store. Beth's hair never did well in the rain. She hated to waste a good hair day running from the car to the store, but it was too late now. She should have said no. Maybe she never should have said "I do."

As Nick pulled up to the front doors of the huge store, he reached back to the seats behind them.

"Here's your umbrella, Beth. I know you don't like your hair to get wet."

"Thanks." She knew she should say more, but she was too upset.

In the store, Nick asked her twice if there was anything else she wanted. He didn't say a word when she placed her outrageously expensive hair products in the cart. She'd always thought her hair was her best feature, and Nick knew it, so he didn't complain.

That evening Nick picked a movie for them. As they

watched it, Beth realized it wasn't the kind of movie Nick preferred at all. But she kept quiet. When she felt chilly, she rubbed her upper arms but didn't say anything. Nick walked to the thermostat and turned up the heat. He grabbed a blanket for her and took his sweater off, leaving himself in just a T-shirt.

When the movie with the happy ending was over, Beth's face was wet with tears. She began to cry.

"What's wrong? You haven't been yourself all day." Nick waited for her to answer.

"I read an article."

Nick didn't speak for a bit. This wasn't the first time a magazine article had ruined a perfectly fine day.

After a long minute, he answered gently, "What was it this time? 'Ten Ways to Tell your Husband Is a Louse?' or 'Five Ways to Discover if He's Lying to You?' Or was it 'Six Reasons It's Time to End Your Perfectly Fine Marriage?'"

"Ten Signs of a Healthy Marriage," she said.

"Are *you* glad we're married?" Nick asked. "Are you okay with us? That's all that matters. Not what some single New York City journalist with a looming deadline thinks."

He walked over and kissed her on the forehead. "It's getting late, and I'm tired. Will you stick with me for another night?"

She smiled, and he reached out to take her hand and pull her up. As he did, she felt a strong urge to give him a long hug, but since he wasn't the hugging sort, she contented herself with holding hands as they walked down the hall to their bedroom.

The Choir Director's Daughter

Sophia Hanson took special notice of Layla Lehman as she passed her in the hallway on her way to Mr. Fisk's physics classroom. The two girls had lived in the same town all their lives. Sophia met Layla in kindergarten, but she never really saw her until today. The evening before, her mother mentioned something about Layla that grabbed Sophia's attention.

Sophia's favorite class is concert choir, but she loves physics too. She likes all her classes and loves school in general.

In choir, Layla sits in the back row on the end. Everyone knows Layla made the audition-only choir because her mother serves as director. Layla sings in tune and prepares well, but her voice sounds thin and breathy.

All the students adore Mrs. Lehman. Sophia assumes the students realize Layla is part of the package. Sophia never hears other students complain that Layla doesn't belong. Nobody ever says anything about her, good or bad.

Layla's mother has the reputation as the best choir director in the state. The school knows it's lucky to have her. Their concert choir competes in every available competition and always achieves the highest marks.

Choirs are a big deal at Springfield Dairy High School. Its football, basketball, and baseball teams rank well below average. None of the SDHS sports teams ever make it to the playoffs, but the audition-only choir wins everything.

The SDHS Booster Club does its best to earn funds to support bus transportation and entry fees for every competition into which Mrs. Lehman has the energy to enter the choir, and Mrs. Lehman possesses boatloads of energy.

The night before, at the dinner table, Sophia's mother had said, "Have you ever noticed Mrs. Lehman's appearance?"

"I see her almost every day at school, Mom. She always looks terrific. She's the best dressed teacher at school by far. Kids comment all the time that she never seems to wear the same clothes twice."

"I believe it. Do you notice her manicured nails and her highlighted hair?"

Sophia nodded. "She always looks awesome."

"What about Layla in the back row on the end? She seems like a quiet girl. Have you ever seen her looking well-groomed? Does her hair ever look nice? Have you ever noticed what she wears?"

"No." Sophia realized she hadn't noticed or thought about it.

"Does she have any friends at school? I've never seen any kids talk to her. At the reception after your last concert, her mother circled around to greet the families. I noticed Layla sitting alone at a table in the corner by herself the whole time. As I passed by, I talked to her for a couple of minutes. She seems really shy. I was wondering if you could give some thought and see what you can do to help her?"

Sophia shrugged. She didn't want to commit to anything. Still, she decided to keep her eyes open in case an opportunity hit her on the head.

"It catches my attention when a mother consistently dresses smart, and her kids walk around unkempt. It seems like Mrs. Lehman spends money freely on her own appearance but hasn't given a thought to her daughter's. Mothers like that grab my attention. And not in a good way. I have nothing against Mrs. Lehman getting manicures or buying clothing, but why doesn't she take her daughter with her once in a while?"

Sophia rubbed the back of her neck. "I suppose that would cost twice as much."

"I'm a mother, and I can tell you that most moms want better for their children than they have for themselves. I hope you'll keep that in mind when you're raising my grandchildren, young lady."

Sophia shrugged as if she didn't care, but she heard the words and mulled them over as they finished their salmon, potatoes, and asparagus in silence.

These Happy Golden Years

Betsy pulls her car into the parking space closest to the front door of the Golden Years facility. Without exception, one of the seven spots of the small visitor lot nearest the sliding front doors is always available. Her car is sometimes the only one in the lot. Many afternoons when she pulls up, it's just her car and her dad's.

She greets the woman at the front desk by name as she signs in. Betsy was here earlier but left to pick up dinner at a nearby drive-through. She walks through the main cafeteria adjacent to the lobby, then down a long hallway. She once counted twenty-two rooms off the hall.

The door to every room along the hallway is propped open. She recognizes most of the people. She's passed by these rooms many times. Betsy wonders how she would feel if strangers walked by her room and looked in. Even though she values privacy, she can't resist glancing in while passing by.

At seven o'clock in the evening, dinner is long past. Some of the residents in the rooms along the hallway sit in chairs watching television. Some lie in bed with their lights out. Not a single resident entertains a visitor. In the weeks she's come to spend time with her mother, Diana, she's never witnessed a visitor in any of the rooms along that particular hallway.

After she passes the twenty-second room, she cuts right through the corner of a secondary cafeteria, turns right again, and arrives at her mother's room, the third door on the right. This newer section of the building contains two blocks of rooms. Each block of nine rooms surrounds a small living-room-like seating area. Thankfully, her mother was placed in this newer section where the rooms are more privately situated.

When Betsy helped her mother move in, one of the workers walked the two of them next door to room 335 to introduce them to Delores. Betsy and her mom were encouraged by the visit. A colorful tablecloth on the tiny round table in Delores's room served as a friendly focal point. Bright-colored pictures hung on all four walls.

Delores wore a beautiful paisley top and looked as if her hair had been recently styled. Betsy hoped she and her mother might become friends. She realized that Delores needed to pass by room 333 any time she left her own room. Betsy imagined future meals where Delores stopped by to pick up her mother on her way to lunch or dinner. Her end room sits adjacent to the storage closet where they keep supplies such as paper goods, mops, and cleaning products. Being at the end is good for peace and quiet, but Betsy thinks it might not help Delores's social life.

On a day right after Diana moved into the assisted living facility to rehab after surgery and a serious infection, a visitor arrived for Delores. She left the building with the visitor for a couple of hours. But since that day, now weeks ago, Betsy and her dad have never seen another person visit Delores. And to their great disappointment, Delores eats all of her meals alone in her room.

In fact, they've only witnessed two of the other residents on this side of the facility have a visitor since that day. Both came on Sunday afternoons.

One of the residents on the far side of the sitting area across from room 333 had a visitor once on a Sunday afternoon. Betsy didn't want to stare, so she wasn't sure who visited, but two weeks later, her mother saw the resident of that room removed in an ambulance. The following week the room was empty—a new resident moved in not long afterward. Betsy asked one of the staff nurses about the situation, but she said she couldn't share confidential information about the other residents.

A man living in the block on the other side of the small cafeteria had a woman visit him once. They spent most of the afternoon walking around the two blocks together. Since he walked so well, Betsy assumed the man regained his strength enough to move back home after hip or knee surgery.

Her mother dislikes being alone at this strange place. She's not herself as a result of the infection. Her wound is healing, but progress is slow. Betsy visits almost all weeknights and most Sunday afternoons. She's been granted a three-month leave from her part-time job. Betsy brushes her mother's hair most nights. They share the news of their days. At seven o'clock, Diana likes to watch two of her favorite game shows. Betsy watches them with her.

Friends from Diana's church usually visit her on Saturdays, so Betsy drives to her own home every Saturday, washes clothes, and repacks her suitcase. She drives back to her parents' town on Sunday afternoons and wheels Diana down two long hallways for a treat at the coffee shop. On the way back to room 333, they stop and watch the birds in the ceiling-high birdcage off the cafeteria. Her mother used to love to sit on her back patio and watch birds. She can identify many by their songs.

Diana's husband, long retired, arrives every morning before nine o'clock. He brings her the daily newspaper and any mail she receives. They spend each morning and afternoon together. If she happens to have a physical therapy appointment, her husband accompanies her. He says, "Well done." She's proud to have him there. No one else's family visits when they do their exercises.

Betsy's siblings both live more than five hundred miles away. Her sister flew up one week to keep Diana company. Betsy took several days to go home, get caught up with chores, and rest. Her dad kept his regular schedule. Her sister even stayed overnight twice in their mother's room, resting in a recliner. But after a week, her responsibilities beckoned her back home.

A basket on Diana's nightstand is filled with letters and cards she's received from people in her church and from her sister. Since her illness, her sister writes at least once a week. She fills Diana in on all the easy-going family news from two states away. She encourages her sister to maintain a good attitude and follow the instructions from her health care providers.

Most nights, Betsy waits until her mother falls asleep before she leaves. Diana becomes distraught at bedtime, so Betsy tells her mother she'll stay until she falls asleep, but then she really needs to go and get some sleep herself.

As she quietly leaves the building, she sometimes passes one or two of the staff members and waves goodbye to them. When she makes her way down the long hallway, all the doors are open at least partway. Every resident lies in bed. One man's television is always on, but the rest of the residents lie in quiet rooms with the overhead lights out.

The front lobby desk sits empty, so she moves by without stopping. Betsy wraps her coat snuggly around her as she steps into the cold winter night. Her car is the only vehicle in the small visitor parking lot. No surprise. Betsy is thankful she doesn't have to walk far, especially since the parking lot surface is slippery from the recent snowfall.

She calls her husband to check in as she drives the twenty minutes to her dad's house. Her husband is holding down the fort at home. Thankfully their kids are grown, so she's able to be there for her mom. She and her dad have the tag-teaming down. He arrives in the morning, drives home for lunch, and then returns in the afternoon. Betsy joins him by four o'clock, and her dad leaves for home about an hour later. Until Diana regains her strength and is physically ready to move back home, they want her to know she isn't alone.

Powers of Concentration

Tara enjoys getting lost in new worlds when she reads. She prefers realistic stories set in towns or countries that she's never visited. She doubts she'll ever travel much, and stories satisfy her mild case of wanderlust. Characters living out their lives, interacting with each other in fresh settings—that's what she loves.

When she was young, she would often sit on the couch in the middle of the living room, book in hand and a faraway look on her face. If anyone in her family spoke to her while she read, she might not even notice. Her mother said her strong ability to concentrate would serve her well one day.

When Tara had that faraway look on her face, and her mother wanted her attention, she touched Tara on the shoulder, and the world of the book would fall away. A quick punch on the arm was her brother's method. Her younger sister Gracie didn't understand why her sister didn't answer her. Gracie often felt hurt and ignored by her sister. Tara's mother always said Gracie would make a great mom because she heard and noticed everything.

Her mom was right. Gracie's four young children are happy and well cared for. Tara's brother works as a prosecutor for a state on the east coast. Tara teaches high school English.

Tara recently moved to a different state to teach at a new, prestigious school. Away from family for the first time in her life, she longs to find friends soon. She's heard from the principal at her new school that she has a lot in common with the choir director. The choir director just moved from out of state also.

Twice, when the two teachers passed each other in the hall, Tara greeted her, but Katherine looked straight ahead with a faraway look on her face. Tara isn't sure if the woman ignores her on purpose or if she should tap her on the shoulder.

Locked In

"C ourtney! You still in here?"

Teresa grabbed the bottom of the bathroom door and shook it. She tried to turn the lock in both directions for the twentieth time, to no avail. The ladies' room was crowded and noisy now, in between movie times. She texted her daughter, then tried to call her, but received no response. While waiting in line for the restroom, they'd agreed whoever finished first would go ahead to the theater to find their seats and meet the other one there. Courtney had probably silenced her phone in the theater.

The restroom crowd thinned out after five minutes. The place wasn't as noisy anymore. Maybe now she could get someone's attention.

"Hello! I'm stuck in here. Can someone get an employee? Hello!"

She shook the door. No one responded to her pleas. Teresa heard a faucet running. On the other end of the line of stalls, a door closed. Someone in the room cleared their throat. The automatic dryer ran, then stopped.

"Hello! Could someone get a manager? I'm stuck in here." Bending down and looking right and left, she could tell the nearby stalls were empty. She peeked out through the cracks and couldn't see anyone in the aisle, but she knew she wasn't alone in the room.

Teresa waited another minute. She resigned herself to the inevitable, pulled out some paper toilet seat covers, and spread them over the floor. The floor teemed with all sorts of horrible germs, no doubt. She eased herself down and considered how to wriggle out. She attempted feetfirst but changed her mind. Shifting her body around, Teresa began to squirm out headfirst.

"Mom! What's going on? Let me help you. I was wondering where you were. Give me your hands."

Teresa stood up and brushed herself off vigorously. Looking up toward the sink area, she noticed two women holding their phones. They faced her direction. Startled, she realized the two were recording her. She pivoted to face away from the cameras, but another woman stood leaning against the wall. She also pointed a phone in

Teresa's direction to record her, the same as the other two women.

Teresa wanted nothing more than to wash her hands thoroughly, but instead, with head down, she bolted toward the door and strode as fast as she could go toward her car. Twenty yards out from the bathroom, she turned around to make sure her daughter was following her. When Courtney jogged and caught up with her, Teresa said, "Sorry Court. I know we've been talking about seeing a movie together for months, but I need to go home."

"Mom, you're limping."

"I think I pulled something with my under-the-door maneuver. It doesn't feel serious. How about coming home, and we can watch a movie there? We'll pick up whatever food you want on the way home. Sorry to ruin our theater night."

"What happened?"

"The door wouldn't open, and I had trouble getting help. Thanks for coming back. I pounded on the door and called for help. I mean, how did those women know I wasn't eighty years old or seriously ill? Or what if my leg were in a cast? I couldn't have crawled out then. Your generation is unbelievable."

"It probably looked funny to them."

"It wasn't funny."

"Anyway, it's not just my generation. I think that woman by the wall was close to forty. Maybe even fifty. Why didn't you say something to them? You should have said something. You know, you can give a pretty impressive lecture when you want to, Mom."

"They had cameras on me."

"Yeah, I guess. They wanted a show, and one of your lectures would have made an awesome show."

When the two arrived at Teresa's house, she gave her husband a twenty-second summary. David poured his wife and daughter each a glass of wine while Teresa took a quick shower and Courtney checked on her toddler. The three met back in the family room.

"I got the baby to sleep a few minutes ago," David said. "Grandpa has the magic touch, if I do say so myself. If you two want to try your luck again sometime, I'm up for babysitting."

"Thanks, dear. I'm not sure I'll ever go to a theater again, but we're going to watch a movie here tonight if that's okay."

"Perfect. I have work to do anyway. First, should we do a search to see if we can find a video of my beautiful wife crawling gracefully out from under a public bathroom stall? We could make a race of it."

"Don't you dare. If it's out there, I don't want to know about it. I just want to forget."

While mother and daughter watched a movie together, David spent time searching but was unable to find a video of his wife in the theater restroom. The next day, Courtney did find one but never shared it with anyone, especially her mother.

Credit Card Catastrophe

Birds sang with early spring energy. The day began sunny and pleasant. But by afternoon, the mail had been delivered, and with the contents of the mail, dark clouds formed. Rain fell, and life seemed hopeless.

Maybe Megan was being melodramatic. It wouldn't be the first time, as those who knew her well could testify. But she had replaced sleep with worry for more hours than she cared to count, dreading the arrival of this particular mail delivery. Now that the bill had arrived, she knew there was no way out. She would need to tell Brian. There was no other option.

If only her parents lived closer. She might have gone to them in secret and asked for help. They would have been willing and able, she knew, but they would have insisted she confess to Brian. Wisconsin and Minnesota seemed worlds apart to her today, and there was no one nearby she knew well enough to turn to for help. She and Brian were alone in their new Packer-loving Dairy State. *Poor Brian. How will I tell him?*

Megan opened the junk mail first and tossed it all in the recycling bin. She used her letter knife to slit open her birthday card from Mom and Dad. When she removed the card from the envelope, a crisp one-hundred-dollar bill slid out onto the table. Megan burst into sobs. It would take a lot more than one hundred dollars to solve her problem.

With a sick feeling in her stomach, she opened the dreaded credit card bill. Using her phone, Megan calculated it would take more than two hundred fifty of the Benjamin Franklin currency notes to rid her of her debt.

Megan paid the minimum amount due each month on her credit card. She never missed a payment. Her mistake was continuing to use the card until the interest due each month crept to its now-unmanageable amount. Poor Brian. He had no idea. And Megan was afraid to tell him. She dreaded seeing the look of disappointment on his face. He already worked so hard.

What would they do? She wouldn't mind working, but with a new baby and two little kids at home who needed her, it didn't make sense for her to look for work. She had never been able to earn much back when she worked in retail anyway. And besides, Brian's unpredictable travel schedule was tough enough to cope with and manage life around. She knew her limits. They knew their limits.

It wasn't as if she were on drugs or had a gambling problem. And it wasn't as if she had a shopping addiction. Anyone who looked in her closet could testify that she didn't spend much on clothes. Or shoes. Or handbags. They didn't eat out often. She didn't run to Starbucks every morning. Things were just tight.

Money always seemed tight. It wasn't enough that she shopped for clothes at garage sales and secondhand shops. The little things added up fast. Payday never seemed to come soon enough. Megan charged a pack of diapers here, a tank of gasoline there, the occasional load of groceries, and now all of a sudden, they owed $27,000.

Maybe it was having an infant and a toddler in diapers at the same time, she thought. It wasn't as if they had even planned to have a third baby. It just happened.

Her father kept telling her that when a couple is married, there are no accidents. His words did make her feel better, but with the third baby came the need for a larger vehicle. And now, with depreciation, the amount owed in payments on the car was greater than its current value.

It wasn't as if they could have ignored the doctor co-pays or waited for a few years to replace the worn tires. Life was expensive, and it seemed there was always something.

So today was the day. When Brian arrived home, she would settle the kids in front of the television. She would tell him with the baby in her arms to soften the delivery a bit.

But Brian came home early that day, and he caught her with red eyes. As soon as he asked her what was wrong, she burst into tears again. Before she had a chance to begin her well-rehearsed speech, the facts burst out between ridiculous sobs. In less than ninety seconds, Brian had the whole story.

Early the next morning, while she was feeding the baby, he gave her a quick kiss and told her they'd talk that night. He might have a plan, he said.

Men! How in the world could he have a plan already? Last night, they had been busy feeding the kids, bathing them, and getting them to bed. By the time the kitchen was cleaned and toys were picked up, Brian said he was tired. And by the time Megan took her shower and crawled into bed, Brian was asleep. Megan knew for sure he had slept because she had been awake all night tossing and fretting and praying. How in the world could he have a plan already when he was sleeping all night?

That night, by five o'clock, Megan had Brian's favorite dinner started. She hoped he would come home. What if he didn't? What would she do then?

But Brian did arrive home right on time with a smile on his face. Megan took a deep breath, and when she saw his expression, she released a day's worth of tension in a rigorous sigh. During dinner, the kids were more quiet than usual, so Brian shared his plan.

"First, I want you to know that we are both in this together. We probably shouldn't have laid the burden of paying the bills on your shoulders. I know you didn't want the job. Or maybe we should have been involved together with it. Anyway, maybe we should share the job of paying the bills for a while.

"Secondly, we might just have to swallow our pride and admit we need help. There's nothing I can come up with to get out of this on our own. With my work schedule, it's just not possible for me to get a second job. I have most weekends off, but I need to be available. That's just the job. You know how it is. Our friends and your family are back in Minnesota, and we haven't been here long enough to make good friends. It takes time. That's just how life is when you move to a new state, I guess.

"Here's my thought. Why don't you call your parents and see if they'd be willing to let you and the kids stay with them for a while? At least until we pay the balance down enough for the payments and interest to be more reasonable. There's a single guy at work I'm getting to know. I'll see if he'll let me sleep on his couch for a while. He travels more than I do, so I have a feeling he might not mind. If that doesn't work, I'll get the cheapest room I can find. We can give notice on our lease tomorrow. You pack up what you need for you and the kids, and we can put our furniture in storage. On weekends I'll drive up and visit. It's only five hours. We'll get aggressive about paying off the debt. I think we can do it. What do you think?"

Megan ran over, gave him an enthusiastic hug, and picked up her phone to call her folks, knowing their answer before she even asked. After the call, she felt the warmth of the oven heating up the house, so she opened the kitchen windows to cool herself down. She looked outside and noticed the blue sky for the first time that day, and she listened to the birds sing cheerful melodies.

The White Utility Van

N atalie finished work at seven-thirty each week-
day evening. Often the last to leave the building,
she surveyed the lot before proceeding to her
car, especially on dark autumn evenings like this one.

After unlocking her car door, she spotted the utility
van at the far edge of the lot. Her Mercedes and the van
were the only two vehicles in sight. She closed the car
door behind her as soon as she was inside, pressing the
lock button as fast as possible. She glanced over her shoulder toward the van and didn't notice any movement.
Large vans scared her to death. She blew out a series of
short breaths.

Natalie didn't mind leaving work after everyone
else, as long as hers was the only car in the lot. The

neighborhood was a safe area. Crime in the town was rare. The van made her nervous, though.

The next night after work, the entire lot was empty except for her vehicle and the van. This time, it was parked right next to her car. By the time she became aware of the situation, she'd already turned out the lights and locked the front doors of her workplace.

She froze. All was quiet.

She debated whether to unlock the office building, re-enter, and turn lights on. She could call her boss, but she'd be too embarrassed to bother her. She could call the police. But what if it was nothing?

Natalie decided to hurry out and get it over with. Since the van was parked on the driver's side of her car, she entered from the passenger side, locked the doors, and then with some difficulty, crawled over the middle console. She started her car, threw it in gear, and sped away from the building.

The next two evenings, she closed alone, and the same thing happened. She imagined a man in the van, examining her actions and planning his move. She had read articles on the dangers of parking near utility vans. They were the perfect vehicle for abductions.

With the dark sky and tinted windows, she couldn't tell if anyone was in the van or not. Her fears were cascading out of control. Maybe he had a gun or a knife. Or maybe the van was empty. But why was it parked near her car each night?

Ever since the first evening she spotted the white van, she parked her car in a different section of the small lot each day. Somehow the van kept finding its way next to her vehicle. She was spooked.

After several nights of shaking in terror as she drove away, she decided enough was enough. Natalie sent an email to Human Resources. They responded to her the same day.

According to Colleen from HR, the van was a recent company purchase. The building maintenance employee used it for company business during the workday. His wife gave him rides to and from work, but whenever he took the van out during the day, he'd try to park near the Mercedes when he returned. In his enthusiasm to keep the company van in pristine condition, he thought it least likely to acquire door dings if he parked it next to the nicest car in the lot.

Natalie made a point of parking as near the front doors as possible after receiving the note. Marvin, the building maintenance worker, on advice from HR, began to park the shiny white van in the far corner of the lot, next to the trash bin.

A Simple Substitution

Monica's husband changed her life one evening when he came home from work and told her without warning that he was leaving her. Six weeks later, he brought the reason he left her to their daughter's volleyball game.

Jared and Monica used to sit together and hold hands amid the other parents of her daughter's team. Now, while Monica still sat with the other parents, her husband and his new girlfriend seated themselves near the entrance. Jared didn't greet any of the other parents, and they didn't greet him, but they all noticed him. They said to Monica, "He's an idiot," "I'm so sorry," and "We have no idea what he sees in her."

Monica's closest volleyball-mom friend said to her, "I

told Jess he'd be sleeping on the couch all week if he said one word to your ex or his girlfriend. Maybe a little silent treatment will do him some good."

She looked at her husband and watched him holding hands with another woman. She said, "He's not my ex. We're separated. He just moved out after twenty years of marriage. He's not my ex. He's just going through some ridiculous sort of crisis."

Monica fretted every night about what she'd do if he asked if he could come back. She wanted the chance to find out. She still loved him.

The next week she was served divorce papers. Monica wasn't ready to let Jared go, so she put the papers in a drawer and tried to forget about them. Maybe she'd wake up one morning and this whole nightmare and all its accompanying humiliations would be over.

Several weeks later, her daughter came home from visiting her dad for the weekend. She helped Monica get dinner ready. "Dad says he's going to Mexico in two months to marry Jamie. He bought plane tickets. One for me, two for Jamie's parents, and a bunch more."

Jared and Monica hadn't spoken since the day he left. Jared texted her a few times to arrange to have his daughter visit every other weekend. Now they'd fallen into that schedule without paying attorneys or going to court. Monica loved her daughter and wanted her to have her dad in her life, so she wouldn't fight the informal custody arrangements. But she decided she would not make it easy for him to get divorced. It was her marriage too, and she had promised "until death do us part." She didn't plan to make it painless for him to leave her and marry someone else. After more than twenty years of marriage, he owed her.

Two weeks later, she still hadn't opened or signed the divorce papers. Her daughter came home from her dad's and was excited to show Monica her new dress.

"Jamie and I went shopping," she said. "We had a lot of fun. I hope it's okay, Mom. She bought me a dress for the wedding. Jamie said I need to ask you if the dress is okay. I'll try it on and be right back." She yelled as she ran up the stairs so her mom could hear her. "Dad says I can only go if it's okay with you. Can I go, Mom? Jamie's sister says I can stay in her hotel room with her and her two kids. They're just a little younger than me."

As soon as her daughter fell asleep, Monica phoned her friend Anita. Anita's husband, Tony, is an attorney. Monica told Anita she hadn't opened or signed divorce papers.

"You'll need to contest the divorce in court if you want to delay the process," Anita said. "And it might already be too late. Open the papers right away and read the dates." She also strongly advised Monica to see an attorney about custody arrangements.

"I have the trust from my folks that we never dipped into. I'll be fine—I'm not too worried about money. Jared sent me a text the other day saying I can keep the house. Last year, he had a great year at the firm, and we decided to pay off the mortgage, so I'll have a roof over my head. But Charlotte says he's flying to Mexico in six weeks to get married to his girlfriend. I've never signed the papers, Anita. Isn't that bigamy?"

"You'll have to check with an attorney, but Tony says Jared can move forward with the divorce without your signature. Both spouses don't need to sign papers in our state," Anita said.

"I've never heard of such a thing. What an awful law."

"You could do a search and probably verify what I'm saying that way. Of course, Tony advises you to speak with an attorney."

Passenger Viewpoint

The airplane doors closed, no passengers remained standing, and the seat next to Jackie was still empty. She couldn't remember the last time she enjoyed a two-seat row to herself. Such luxury.

After an hour in the air, the pilot broadcasted, "To your left you'll see Center City. In a couple of minutes, Green Lake and the entire chain of lakes will appear on your right."

Jackie loved when pilots made these types of announcements. Why shouldn't a pilot extend himself and provide extra service? She could tell by his voice he was a friendly sort of person. She preferred that type of pilot to a cranky one. His thoughtful broadcasts made the flight more pleasant. Those not interested could use their noise-canceling headphones.

Hearing him speak gave her confidence in his ability. He sounded sober. Jackie once heard that some pilots fly after drinking, and she didn't want that. *Why shouldn't a pilot both fly the plane and provide tourist guide service? He probably finds more satisfaction in his job because he thinks of those he's serving and attempts to add value to their lives,* she thought.

The pilot reminded Jackie of her postal carrier. After fifteen years, Jackie had recently lost her postal carrier Susie to a new route. She'd never have another like her. Susie was the type to stop and chat for a few seconds and ask about her customers' days. Rather than stuff the box with a package that didn't fit and risk ruining the contents, Susie turned off her engine and delivered the package to Jackie's front step. Even on delivery days when Susie seemed rushed, she took the time to smile and wave.

Thoughts of her beloved postal carrier brought Stan Stevens to mind. He owned the five and dime in the small town where Jackie grew up. Kids stopped by the store after school to spend money on candy. He treated them with respect. He asked kids about their day. He got to know them, and when he thanked the students for their business and said goodbye, he'd often say, "Tell your mother I said hello." And he didn't mean anything weird by it.

He liked people, and he liked kids. Everyone knew it, and everyone liked him too.

The pilot's voice sounded over the system again. He kindly suggested all passengers prepare for landing. He thanked them for flying his airline, and Jackie thought she could tell by the tone of his voice that he meant it. The smooth, perfect landing was no surprise.

The following day, Jackie had an appointment scheduled with a new doctor. She hoped the doctor was as good at her job as the pilot had been at his today.

Home Improvement Disputes

B rad and Katie Carr love home improvement shows. They don't have much time for television, but they watch home repair and remodeling shows when they do.

The young couple purchased a fixer-upper, and they're in the midst of their first remodel. Their primary bathroom is the first project they're tackling. A dumpster sits in the driveway, and they pulled out everything in the bathroom, down to the studs. When Saturday started, Katie hadn't realized how tired they'd be by four-thirty in the afternoon.

To celebrate their remodeling progress, she invited both of their mothers over for dinner.

"I can't believe you invited company over in the midst

of our project," Brad said. "Good thing we have a second bathroom."

"It's just our moms, and my mom is bringing all the food. She cooked a big pot roast with vegetables, made a fruit salad, and she's bringing dessert too. She said it's a surprise."

"I hope it's one of her pies. I love her pies."

"You like any dessert."

Katie and Brad cleaned up and changed clothes. Not long after, the doorbell rang, and it was Katie's mom. Brad helped her carry everything to the kitchen. Katie had tidied up the kitchen island, and she worked on setting the table.

"Thanks for feeding us. You know I love your pot roast," Brad said.

"No problem. I'm happy to help. Too bad Katie's dad isn't here. He'd have loved helping with this project. He'd be so proud of the two of you and the work you're doing to make a home and build equity."

The doorbell rang, and Katie invited her mother-in-law in. Once the food was laid out, they filled their plates buffet-style and took seats at the table. Katie and Brad let both mothers in on their plans for the bathroom and the work they'd accomplished so far.

"Brad and I are excited to do the work on our own. We're watching videos and home improvement shows together to try to learn. Having Dad's tools is a huge help."

Katie's mom wiped away a tear but smiled and nodded to her. "It makes me happy you two are using them. Your dad loved his tools."

Brad's mom said, "It sounds like a lot of time and money. Your home looks perfectly fine to me the way it is. It's so interesting to hear kids talk about houses these days. Let's tear down this perfectly fine kitchen because the counter has to be granite. Or, we'll just die if we don't have a gas stove and a new backsplash in the most up-to-date color. We need two sinks for our en suite bathroom and two walk-in closets."

Brad's mom continued. "My mother's family had one outhouse in the backyard for a family of eight, and they survived just fine. I was one of five kids in a house with one bathroom. My mother was thrilled to have indoor plumbing and never once complained. It's a hoot to hear kids nowadays and how they need this luxury and that luxury. They don't know anything about need.

"Your dad, God rest his soul," she said while looking at Brad, "he knew about need. When he was sixteen, their family lived an entire summer off what they grew in their vegetable garden. They lived on potatoes, tomatoes, and carrots for an entire summer. His father finally found work after Labor Day. Things lightened up for them then."

"I'm not sure you ever told me that story," Katie said to Brad.

Brad looked at his mom. "I guess we're just starting out and trying to build equity in the house. If and when we sell the home, if we put sweat into it, we'll build value into it."

"Would anyone like more roast or fruit?" Katie said, trying to lighten the mood with her tone of voice.

"I think there's enough roast there for ten grown men, Katie. A general rule of thumb is four to six ounces per person. I think you may have gone overboard."

"Won't it be nice for them to have the leftovers?" Katie's mother said.

Katie excused herself and ran to their bedroom.

Katie's mother said, "I think it's time I headed home. The pie is on the counter, Brad. Could you serve it up?"

"I've eaten enough for three people tonight. I never eat this much. No dessert for me," Brad's mom said. "I think I'll head out, too. Please thank Katie for the delicious roast, the fruit, and everything. It was nice to get out of the house."

"Katie's mother made the food, Mom. Katie and I worked on the bathroom all day."

"I thought it would be nice for them to have leftovers since they're so busy," Katie's mom said.

"Oh, my goodness. I would never have opened my mouth if I knew. I apologize. I don't know what gets into me."

The Safe

Lauren, I'm sorry to call on short notice, but I'm afraid I don't feel up to coming today. I'll phone to reschedule when I'm doing better, if that's okay. Please apologize to Dr. Steve for me."

Julia hung up the phone. That was over. What a relief. Now she had no more responsibilities for the day. Luckily, she'd called when the receptionist was busy, so she hadn't needed to talk to a live person. She hated to cancel on her chiropractor at the last moment, but she couldn't face the world today.

Now Julia was free to go back to bed and stay in her pajamas for another day. Thankfully, she had the long weekend to try and pull herself out of this funk before she needed to go back to work on Tuesday. Today was day two. So far, this spell had cost her only one employee sick day since her office was not open on Saturdays. Usually, these d & d spells, as she called them, lasted only two or three days.

Over the years, she figured out a few tricks—there were things she could try when discouragement and depression came upon her. Usually, one of them would work. Someday she might get around to talking to her physician about medication. However, she hated to take prescription medicine if she could avoid it.

When Julia experienced days like this, she preferred to retreat from everyone and be alone. She supposed it was her pride that kept her in seclusion—not wanting anyone seeing her like this. Julia didn't want to drag anyone else down.

I'll keep to myself, she thought. *Besides, no one really cares about me anymore anyway.* Now that my husband is gone and my parents are gone, I'm alone in the world. For the first time in a long while, she let herself cry.

In the midst of her most recent bout, she somehow mustered the strength to take all her collectibles out of her curio cabinet. Her mother, who suffered similar periods of gloom throughout life, had once mentioned it as a trick that worked for her.

Julia washed and dried each item, dusted the shelves, and put everything back. Collecting was her hobby.

She found such pleasure in handling every item and remembering how she'd come to possess each particular piece. If ever she forgot, she had it all written down. Every object of her collection brought back a memory of a birthday, an anniversary, or a Christmas. Until the shop went out of business around the time of Tim's death, whenever her husband asked her what she wanted, she'd always say, "Go to Treasurable Collectibles and ask for Jean. She knows exactly what I like. If Jean isn't there, then ask for Irene."

Just as Julia hoped, each time she handled an item, she was transported back to the holiday or the birthday when she opened the gift. Before long, Julia found that the process of remembering happy times helped wash away her melancholy feelings.

During another spell, she devoted a full day to watching comedies. After coming across an article espousing the benefits of laughter on health, she'd searched for humorous shows and movies. Julia sat alone that day, watching television, trying to recall what it might feel like to laugh. Eventually, the comedies distracted her from her gloom. She found herself smiling, and then after a time, laughing. Laughing felt good.

When Tim was alive, he played music for her when she felt down. He knew just what to play to reach her. Sometimes he'd serenade her with her favorites, and then

he'd throw a love song in with the perfect lyrics. She ac-
cused him over the years of not having a romantic bone
in his body, but he proved his love for her over and over
in the way he treated her and the things he did for her.

Today, she decided if she found the strength to drag
herself out of bed, she was going to try art. Julia was in
the mood for the Impressionists. She'd grab a stack of
her art books from the bookshelf downstairs and sit at the
kitchen table with Monet, Cassatt, Renoir, and Morisot.
Maybe beauty would give her a boost.

She did want to feel better but just didn't have much
energy. Her foggy brain couldn't even consider tackling
the chore of reading a book. On healthy days, she loved
a good thriller, a self-help book, or a romance, but she
knew she wouldn't be able to focus today. However, she
did think she could muster the strength to look at some
art. Art might be just the thing.

In the middle of the afternoon, when she realized
she wasn't finding success with her favorite Impressionist
painters, she remembered she needed to head downstairs
to the safe to search for the title to her car. It was time to
shop for a vehicle, and she would need the title to trade
hers in for a new model. Before he had passed away, on
one of his good days, Tim bought her a new car and the
oil change package that accompanied it.

He had advised her to continue the tradition they had

of selling her automobile when it hit 100,000 miles. She could comfortably afford the expense, and he encouraged the plan from a safety perspective.

Tim traveled often for work when he was alive, and over the years, he insisted on the trade-ins at the six-digit mark. "I don't want you driving to and from work or zooming around on the expressway all alone in an unreliable car when I'm halfway around the world."

And that was that. He'd looked out for her and cared for her in a myriad of ways when he was alive. But now it was time to find the title and shop for a car by herself for the first time. She dreaded the thought. She'd never felt more alone.

Before it turned dark, she trudged downstairs to hunt for the title. She hated to go to the basement in the dark. She always had, even when Tim was alive. So, two hours before sunset, she headed down. The heavy safe rested in the back corner of a closet on top of a metal filing cabinet. She opened the safe and made three trips to transfer all the contents from the safe to the sofa in the downstairs family room. The lighting was better near the sofa than in the closet, and she could sit comfortably while she worked.

Next to her now on the sofa sat two tall stacks of paperwork, each almost a foot high. The piles included paid-off mortgages and closing papers for homes they'd owned, stocks, financial papers, and purchase agreements for every car they'd ever bought. Julia located the title that had started this search in the first place, and she set it aside. Then she continued looking through the papers.

Sometime before Tim's death, she had gone through the safe and cleared out dated papers, including the wills for each one of their parents, who had all passed away before Tim became ill. But now, relaxed on the family room sofa and in no hurry, she sorted and organized papers.

She bundled the car papers together. She only owned one car, but she couldn't bear to destroy the purchase papers of the other vehicles she and Tim spent time in together. She bundled the stocks together and the papers from their financial advisor. And there were the estate papers the attorney sent to her after Tim passed away. Since they had no children, the entire estate was left to her.

But then, she came upon the papers in the bottom half of one of the stacks. To be honest, she rarely thought about most of these, and some she was unable to remember at all. She could not even recall signing power of attorney papers for her brother or her sister-in-law. Or the power of attorney papers for her two sisters and their spouses.

Since all the children of her two younger sisters were still minors, she had the wills and the papers transferring custody to her in the event of her sisters' untimely deaths. And her friend Susan and her husband had selected her as guardian of their children also.

In fact, after she counted all her nieces and nephews and children of friends she had been asked to raise, she'd counted thirteen children. To the best of her ability, she estimated their current ages to be between seven and seventeen years old.

Julia began to laugh. As she imagined her fifty-five-year-old self raising thirteen children, her laughter grew to hilarity. Of course, when her friends and family named her in their wills as their children's guardian upon death, Tim had been alive and well. She wondered if the papers would be legally binding anymore, but as she read through them, she noticed the language "Tim and/or Julia" used, and she concluded it was likely the papers were legally binding. She laughed again, imagining trying to house and raise thirteen children, half of whom were now hormonal teenagers.

Theoretically, Julia knew there was a possibility some tragic event might deliver the baker's dozen to her home, but she knew it was extremely unlikely. With a smile on her face, she resolved to move forward with her life and place her hope against any and all tragic events.

She and Tim would have loved to have their own children early in their marriage, but after the doctor crushed their hopes, they made the decision to accept their inability to have children and move forward together with their family of two.

Julia thought about her friend Karen from church.

She had been a single, thirty-year-old ER nurse, but one day, a car accident in Wausau had taken the life of Karen's brother and sister-in-law. As legal guardian, she quit her job, moved two hours north to Wausau, and lived with her two teenaged nieces, ages fifteen and sixteen.

Julia wondered how Karen was doing now. They'd lost touch, but she imagined Karen had her hands full supporting and raising two teen girls.

Just yesterday, Julia had been lying on her bed in the middle of the afternoon, thinking no one in the world cared for her. She felt completely alone. But after spending an hour or so going through the papers from her safe, she was reminded that many loved her and cared for her. And not only that, she was needed.

Thirteen kids, whether they knew it or not, were relying on her as their backup custodian. That meant their parents were counting on her too. In addition, there were the wills of those who named her as executor of their estate. And the power of attorney papers she'd signed.

Her family and friends were counting on her. She was encouraged that so many relied on her and trusted her with their children and their belongings. Julia went from laughing to sobbing. But she wasn't sobbing for sorrow as she had earlier. She was sobbing for joy. The papers in front of her proved she was still needed, important, and useful.

After wiping her tears with her sleeve, she blew her nose with a tissue she pulled from her pocket. Then, even though sunset approached, Julia took a quick shower and dressed herself for the first time in forty-eight hours. She quickly whispered a thank you to God for helping her out of her funk, and she moved ahead with the rest of her day.

A Change in the Neighborhood

Kara put the boys to bed by eight o'clock. She settled in the family room to watch television until Justin came home. His plane was due to land around ten o'clock, and she expected him home an hour later. Kara often stayed up late, so it was no big deal for her to wait for her husband.

At the anticipated time, Justin came in through the garage door. Before greeting her with his customary kiss, he said, "What's that car sitting out in front of the house?"

"What do you mean?" The family room was at the back of the house, so Kara hadn't looked out the front windows for hours.

"There's a car parked in front of the house. Two men are just sitting in it."

132

"I have no clue. I've been back here since I put the boys to bed. They've been sleeping, and I've been watching a movie."

"I'm going to see what's going on." Justin walked right up to the car and knocked on the driver's side window. A man lowered the window several inches.

Justin said, "Is there something I can do for you?" He noticed binoculars on the laps of both men.

"Yes, we'd like you to go back inside. We're keeping an eye on a nearby house. It would be best if you went back in your home."

Justin noticed the FBI badge hanging from the man's neck and walked back into the house. As he unpacked, he told Kara what the men were doing and what they'd said to him.

The next morning, as they drove to Devil's Lake State Park to take a family hike, they heard a news story on the radio. The FBI made a large drug bust at a house on their street just after midnight.

The house across the street, three doors down, had cars pulling in and out of the driveway at all times of day and night. Because of things they'd observed in the front of the house, they had to limit their children's outdoor activities and monitor them more carefully than normal. Justin and Kara had been considering moving for safety reasons.

"Maybe our problems are solved," Justin said. "We might not have to move after all."

Kara clapped her hands. "We'll have to keep a close eye for a while, but wouldn't it be awesome if we didn't need to move. I love our location and our home."

Shabby Coats Buy Vacations

S tacey opened the door to the garage to rush to her meeting, and cold air hit her hard in the face. She turned back into the house to pull her coat from the front closet. It was the first time in six months she'd needed to grab one. Truth be told, she disliked wearing coats and would avoid them as often as possible. She found she could ignore wearing one for the majority of the year, even in Wisconsin. Her work kept her indoors, and she no longer had a dog to walk.

Her own personal rule, and the one she'd raised her children on, was they never were required to wear a coat. When temperatures dropped below freezing, she made them bring a coat in the car in case of vehicle trouble.

If they were playing outside, once they reached a certain age, she trusted them to be smart enough to make wise choices.

If friends asked Stacey where her coat was, she tried to change the subject. Stacey and her family rarely had colds or the flu, and they were the healthiest family she knew. She attributed some of their hardiness to not over-dressing in cold weather.

Stacey reached into her coat pockets. No tissues. She must have washed the jacket last spring. After she gave the shabby coat a whiff to confirm she'd cleaned it, she tossed it on the passenger seat and raced out for her meeting.

It wasn't unusual for her to talk when she was alone. "Dumpy coat, I have not missed you one bit, but thank you for being here for me today just in case the car breaks down. I wonder if anyone ever notices your mismatched button at the bottom. If I loved you more, I'd stitch those unraveled threads at the pocket. Maybe tonight. After all, a stitch in time and all that."

The Benjamin Franklin idiom reminded her of the time she read his *Poor Richard's Almanac*, the book that gave her the idea to keep her coat for just "one more year" every year. How old was it now? She held it up and exam-ined it as she waited for the red light to turn green. Yes, she'd make do another year. Why not? She had no real fondness for coats, hats, scarfs, or mittens, so she wouldn't waste time, money, or energy shopping for new ones.

Stacey would apply Benjamin Franklin's wisdom to the situation for one more year. "When you incline to have new clothes, look first well over the old ones, and see if you cannot shift with them another year, either by scouring, mending, or even patching if necessary. Remember, a patch on your coat, and money in your pocket, is better... than a writ on your back, and no money to take it off."

Stacey felt the same about her wardrobe. She possessed no great affection for dresses, shirts, slacks, or shoes, so she did her best to make do with what she had. Her friends who lived closer to the poverty line than she spent hours and hours and loads of gasoline as they traveled from store to store, or discount store to second-hand shops, buying up bags of new or used clothing. Stacey marveled at this. She preferred to make do with classic pieces she'd purchased five or ten years ago. She supposed she came by it naturally.

A certain evening came to mind. Her mother was going out on a rare date with her father. Stacey complimented her mom on how beautiful she looked (and she did look beautiful). Her mother smiled as she held her arms out to her side and twirled around. "I've had this black dress for over ten years, but why not? It still works."

She thought of her friend Nell. Stacey saw Nell every week at church and once a month at their quilting club meetings. Nell never wore the same thing twice. It took Stacey years to notice. A friend mentioned she couldn't believe Nell didn't have money to go away with them to the quilters convention they all were eager to attend, but she could wear different clothes every day of her life.

About a year ago, after Stacey's friend Debbie mentioned Nell's extensive wardrobe, Stacey started keeping a casual record. After taking notes a short while, she confirmed that each time she saw her, Nell was wearing a different combination of clothing. She did see the occasional slacks repeated, but she wouldn't have recognized them if she hadn't taken notes.

Stacey would never admit she took notes. She was just tired of Nell's "poor me" comments. Nell had a knack for making annoying comments. "I love your car. You're so lucky! Or I'm so jealous of the trips you've made!"

When Stacey mentioned she'd been to seventeen countries, Nell said she'd only been to two in her typical self-pitying way. "Whoopee. Canada was such a hoot."

Stacey wanted to tell Nell that she could travel too if she didn't spend a quarter of her income on clothing, shoes, and outerwear. The two knew very well that their family incomes were similar. Nell just loved those "poor me" digs.

Two years ago, when Stacey pulled up to Nell's house in her new vehicle, her friend complimented it and then turned the conversation over to her own vehicle. It was ten years old, and the rear door on the passenger side no longer worked. Of course, Nell's kids were grown and out of the house, so Stacey wondered out loud how often it mattered.

Stacey wished she'd been brave enough to say, "If you sold a portion of your shoe collection, you'd be able to afford a new door for your vehicle." Stacey knew that Nell made one choice over another, but she wished Nell would admit it rather than deliver her passive-aggressive insults.

When Stacey mentioned her frustration with Nell's comments, Debbie told her to forget about it. That life is too short to waste energy worrying about how others spend their money.

Of course, a year ago, Stacey wouldn't have known anything about the cost of Nell's clothing, but Debbie's comments dropped smoothly into her ears. Each time, Stacey went home and received a further online education to supplement Debbie's tutoring. Before that, she had no idea it was possible to spend so much on clothing. Debbie pointed out the brands Nell wore and how to identify them. The prices flabbergasted Stacey. Stacey told herself she had little interest, and yet, she kept taking notes whenever she saw Nell.

Of course, no one could ever accuse Stacey of being frugal. Her husband can attest to the veracity of that statement. She's just learning that people have their own interests and their own things they're willing to be frugal about. She and her husband share an interest in travel and cars, and she adores her knickknacks, but clothing holds little interest for her.

Stacey abhors Nell's little digs about her cars and her vacations. That's all. She refuses to give Nell the satisfaction of complimenting her on her appearance, even though she always looks nice. And she won't be dropping an "I wish I could have half the wardrobe you have" sort of comment next time she sees her either. Stacey has her dignity.

A Restroom for Hailey

Hailey pulled into the restaurant parking lot faster than she knew she should. Before she could shift her truck into park, hop out of her pickup, and place her boots on the asphalt, the outside lights of the best hamburger place in town went out.

"Oh no!" She lowered her chin, closed her eyes, and let out a long sigh. She had missed the finest restroom in town by a minute. Less than one minute. If only she hadn't had to lunge the extra horse tonight. She would have made it in time if not for that.

Tacos for dinner again tonight. She supposed she would grow tired of them if she kept up this routine, but for now, they still ranked first on her list of favorite comfort foods. Maybe she'd try something else from the menu to keep things fresh. Unfortunately, the restroom at the taco place wasn't the best. The floor was downright dirty, and their hand dryer hadn't worked in decades. Even so, it beat the bathroom back at the barn by a mile. *Anything to avoid that place*, she thought, as she backed out of the parking stall and headed for the budget-friendly taco spot.

Oh, what she would give for a personal toilet that worked. Since the day she had hauled her horse from Wisconsin to Texas to start work at what she hoped would be her dream job, she had put up with the tiny on-location apartment.

Living on the property did have its perks. Hailey could roll out of bed at five-fifty in the morning and be hard at work in the barn by six o'clock. She loved that. Free rent was a huge draw, too, considering her modest wages. Unfortunately, within one week, as spring warmed the area, she discovered that pests overran her tiny unit. Before long, she developed the habit of driving the four miles to town for fast-food meals. Gnats, insects, and mice seemed to find their way into any food she brought home.

Even frozen dinners lost their appeal after she discovered evidence of vermin life on her clean dishes. Her kitchen wasn't much. It consisted of a dorm-sized refrigerator, a single burner, and a small sink. There were no cupboards to store clean dishes in, so she stacked them atop the two-foot-wide counter space.

When Hailey first moved in, the toilet and shower worked. She grew fond of her little apartment off the riding arena, which was run by one of the best reining trainers in the country. The year prior, she had watched videos of his award-winning rides from a thousand miles away and admired his abilities. Now, here she was, a northern girl down in Texas, working as his assistant trainer. At least, she was hired as his assistant trainer. In actuality, she did little more than the work of saddler and warm-up rider. So far. Little by little, the boss showed confidence in her and increased her riding responsibilities.

Her parents insisted she try to find another apartment when they heard pests overran her place. They even helped make inquiries from a distance. With only three apartment buildings in the small town, options were limited. No vacancy would be available for at least another three months. Hailey wasn't sure she could hold out that long.

Every time it rained, her toilet stopped working, and her shower drained at a trickle. This happened to be a year of record-breaking rainfall in Texas, and the wet weather refused to let up. All across the state, flooding wreaked havoc.

She could deal with taking brief showers, but the lack of a toilet was a challenge. She'd been raised with access to functioning indoor toilets and found she was quite fond of the luxury. Using the barn toilet meant crossing the entire indoor arena, then walking outside, rain or shine, in daylight or darkness, to the far side of the barn. The several men who worked on the property used the barn toilet, and she wasn't sure who cleaned it—if anyone ever did. She knew she didn't want the task.

As she sat in the parking lot that evening, eating her taco salad, Hailey planned the next day's lunch break. Choosing from the four eating establishment options in town, she decided it was time for the sandwich shop. Their restroom consisted of a single stall, but she could count on its cleanliness. Tomorrow night, if the boss let her off in time, she planned to make it to the burger place.

She allowed her mind to wander to the three roomy stalls, the immaculate tile flooring, the scented soap, and the air-conditioning. What bliss. Their surplus of moderately plush toilet paper beckoned her to set up camp as long as needed. She daydreamed of asking if they had a rollaway cot she could use, then she chuckled out loud.

Hailey finished her taco salad as she listened to country music on the radio. *Yet another meal alone in my truck,* she thought. Then she realized she was slouching, and she pulled herself up tall and straight.

"First things first," Hailey said aloud. "First I survive this bathroom crisis. Then I figure out how to make a friend or two in this new state in spite of all the hours I work."

She started her pickup and drove back toward the ranch. No matter what, tomorrow Hailey would do her best to make it to the burger restaurant before closing time.

Red Light Rests

The smell of an orange could initiate a full-blown panic attack. This was getting ridiculous. Tina needed to figure something out. She could still picture her student Aaron in her rearview mirror, peeling an orange and sharing half with his brother, as if it were yesterday. But it's been more than seven years. The other three children ate snacks in the car, too, but it's the smell of the orange she can't forget.

Tina wonders what she can do to make her nightmares stop. In daylight hours, she can ignore it all, not that she shares her dream plots with anyone. But her aggravated symptoms have caused her to realize she's harboring feelings powerful enough to disrupt her life. She isn't sure how to fix the problem.

Paying a therapist is financially out of the question. Besides, she'd have to tell people, and she doesn't want that. *Maybe I'm supposed to learn to say no*, she thinks. Maybe saying no is the lesson she needs to learn before something tragic occurs. Her whole issue might be as simple as learning to say no. Her weakness in that area is no secret. Those close to her tease her about it all the time. She'll give the idea some thought.

Not long ago, she added up the hours it had cost her to drive carpool for the two other families for two full school years. Her time driving for carpool equaled twenty-two full nights of rest per year. No wonder she'd been so tired all the time. During her first two years back teaching after taking a break to be at home with her kids, the preparation hours seemed overwhelming. When heaped upon the responsibilities of her home, her family, and her aging parents, Tina thinks it's a wonder she survived.

"As long as you're heading that way, could you swing around and pick up my kid?" they'd said.

Saying no to the other families who asked her to drive their children had not even crossed her mind. As if there would be no cost to her and her family. She blamed her pesky guilt feelings, but she was coming to realize she might have a problem with pride too. She liked to help people. Maybe, though, it had more to do with pride and wanting others to think well of her. She can see now that the other families took advantage of her, but she hadn't realized it at the time.

Instead of staying at school to work on grading, she needed to choose each day between babysitting the carpool kids in her classroom after school as she graded papers or hauling her work home at night and staying up after her family went to bed to complete it. The result had been late nights and lost sleep.

It's crazy, Tina thinks. How had she found it easier—leaving home an extra thirty minutes early, picking up children from two families, driving them into Madison to the private school, teaching all day, and driving them home—than to say the word *no*. No wonder she developed the horrible habit of taking mini-naps at stoplights.

Maybe the mini-naps were the root of her trouble now. She remembers being so tired she had to struggle to keep her eyes open until the next traffic light. And not just once or twice. It became a regular routine. Tina enlisted the help of her eldest daughter, who learned to tap her mom's arm from her driver's side rear seat whenever a light turned green.

All five children still live and breathe, so her nightmares seem melodramatic to her. They border on ridiculous, but they won't stop. All these years later, she realizes her subconscious mind must blame herself for putting a car full of young kids at risk.

Then it clicks. She recalls the news story she read a few months ago about a car accident in a nearby city. A mother had been driving her two children and three others home from school. An accident occurred, resulting in a rollover with a tragic ending. She remembers wondering immediately after reading the story if the mom suffered from exhaustion. Maybe the poor mom merely made the mistake of falling asleep while driving carpool before reaching the next stoplight.

Morning Recitations

J anet woke Saturday morning wondering, for the first time in her life, if more of her days lay behind her than in front of her. She'd never stopped to consider it, but this morning the thought lay heavy on her mind as she struggled to get out of bed. She hit the off button on her alarm rather than the snooze and rolled over and closed her eyes. Then, for the first time in her adult life, Janet spent the entire day in bed. The day she made this choice happened to be the first anniversary of the evening her husband had come home from work, announced he was leaving her, packed a bag, and left.

The morning following her full day in bed, her alarm rang, and a struggle commenced. Janet was tempted to spend another day like the previous one. Rather than

149

feeling rested after a day in bed, she felt wearier than ever. Another day in bed sounded like good medicine, but twinges of guilt tugged at her.

"Is this what I was created for? To huddle under blankets and stay warm?"

The words of Cicero spoke to her, clanging louder in her ears than any opposing thought. They drowned out the temptation she suffered to pull the covers over her head and relax in the comfort of her blankets.

Ben Franklin followed right behind with the words, "Lost time is never found again."

She slept alone in the primary bedroom these days. After hearing the words in her head, she spoke the quotations out loud. With a noisy groan, she sat up in bed.

Mrs. Massey, Janet's sixth-grade teacher, had been a stickler for memorizing poetry, speeches, and quotations. Her entire class memorized "Tyger, Tyger, Burning Bright" by William Blake, Robert Frost's "The Road Not Taken," and the first stanzas of Poe's "The Raven." They memorized Shakespeare, William Carlos Williams, and Emily Dickenson together.

Then there was the Gettysburg Address, the Declaration of Independence, and the Preamble to the Constitution. Mrs. Massey was huge on memorization. She especially loved *Bartlett's Familiar Quotations*, which included some of her favorites from Proverbs, Benjamin Franklin, and Cicero.

Still sitting on the edge of her bed, Janet's thoughts took her back to her childhood kitchen. Her mother bustled around the room, making dinner. While Janet recited, her younger sister Jenny held the current memory assignment in her hands, following along with her eyes in order to voice corrections any time Janet made an error. Their mother listened as she prepared dinner. "There's no reason all three of us can't learn while you recite, Janet," her mother often said.

Janet pictured herself seated at her desk in her sixth-grade classroom. She could envision the view of the room from her front-row seat in the second line of desks from the wall. Her mother, citing statistics to Mrs. Massey the first week of school, had appealed to the teacher, requesting Janet be placed in the front row. Apparently, other parents weren't fighting for front-row seats because even though Mrs. Massey regularly rearranged students' seats, Janet remained in the front row every day for the entire year. The seating arrangement strongly motivated her to practice her reciting assignments. She could never hide from Mrs. Massey behind another student's head.

A proverb popped into her mind—though she hadn't thought of it in months. She spoke the words loud and clear, preaching the message to herself. "A little sleep, a little slumber, a little folding of the hands to rest, and poverty will come upon you like a robber, and want like an armed man" (Proverbs 6:10–11).

Janet put her feet on the floor. As she did, she quoted the verse from Psalm 118 she'd been saying each morning all year as her feet touched the floor. "This is the day that the Lord has made. We will rejoice and be glad in it" (Psalm 118:24).

After the psalm, Janet put a smile on her face, though she did not feel at all like smiling. She had read somewhere that if you smile first, then you'll feel like smiling. She wasn't sure whether she believed the saying or not but decided to try it out. If Janet could remember, she would add a smile to her early morning routine, right after reciting the verse from Psalms and putting her feet on the ground. Why not? She could use some smiles in her life. Maybe it would work.

Next, she did ten backward arm circles because her sister told her arm circles help abate morning stiffness. And then, because more of her life existed in the rearview mirror than ahead (unless she lived past the age of ninety-nine), she decided to continue to alter her morning routine by adding a short walk on the treadmill to her list of things to do before breakfast.

Chocolate Chip Cookies

Sutton couldn't stop thinking about chocolate chip cookies. Her husband preferred them above any other dessert, and she had all the ingredients in her pantry. Even though she used to love to bake, she hadn't made them in years. She decided to surprise Seth when he came home from work. Her kids would appreciate them too.

When Sutton and her husband first married, she used to make chocolate chip cookies frequently. Several years later, her husband decided to stop eating sweets. Sutton joined him soon after. The strategy helped them to watch their weight. The couple fell into a cycle of moving in and out of banning sweets. Tight-fitting clothing was usually the motivating factor.

Her youngest daughter arrived home from school. When she smelled the aroma, she discovered the container filled with cookies on the counter. She took two without even asking. "Yum! Mom, it's not Saturday. Did you go to Grandma's?"

Sutton visited her parents each Saturday. Her mother sometimes sent food home for dinner or a plate of home-made treats.

"No, I thought your dad and you kids might enjoy some cookies."

"They taste like Grandma's. Did you really make them?"

"Time for homework. No more cookies till after dinner."

Soon after, her oldest daughter returned home from school.

"Smells awesome in here." She spied the container on the counter and helped herself to one. "You went to Grandma's today?"

"No, I thought your dad and you kids would like some cookies. They're dad's favorite, you know."

"You're kidding, aren't you? Where did you get them, Mom?"

Sutton picked up the cookie jar and cradled it in her arms. "Just for that, no more for you until after dinner. Now get upstairs and work on your homework."

An hour later, Seth walked in the door. He spotted the cookies. "Did you go to your mom's today?"

"No!" She answered less gently than she meant to. "Why does everyone keep saying that?"

"Who's everyone?"

"You. And the girls."

"Thanks for making my favorite." He kissed her on the cheek.

"You're welcome. Just for that, you can have two."

Sutton had already eaten more than she'd planned, but she brought her husband a beverage and joined him at the table while he savored his cookies. They each recounted a brief summary of their uneventful days. When her husband said he was heading upstairs to change his clothes, Sutton said, "Would you stop by and tell your eldest she can come down for one more cookie if she wants? She hurt my feelings earlier, but I suppose denying her a second of the most delicious cookies on earth was a bit harsh."

"They are the most delicious thing I've had in a long while."

She took the lid off the jar and held it out to him.

He shook his head no. "Temptress! I'd better wait until after dinner."

Before he left, she set the jar down and gave him another hug. "I'm glad you're home. By the way, you're grilling tonight. I have the meat and everything else set to go as soon as you're ready."

Reception Desk at the Vet Clinic

Z oe dropped by her mom's house on her way home from work. Her aunt was visiting from Atlanta. Zoe hadn't seen Aunt Kae since Christmas.

Not long after Zoe arrived, her mother suggested she share some of her work stories. Her mom, Tara, enjoyed hearing them so much she said she'd gather them together in a book one day.

"Zoe sometimes calls after work just to vent," Tara said. "I always advise her that a call to her mother is cheaper than paying for therapy."

"Clients have been known to throw poop at me," Zoe said.

"People throw poop at you?" Kae moved from across the room to the chair closest to Zoe.

"Customers have thrown dog poop at me. I mean, it's happened a handful of times."

"No way!"

"Thankfully the poop has been in bags."

Zoe started her story.

"The other day a woman came in. She was in a tizzy, freaking out about her puppy. Good thing the lobby was empty at the time. She kept screaming at the little puppy. The dog had pooped in the car on the way over and poop got all over the leash. She was so upset she couldn't listen to me or answer my questions, so I put her in an exam room before other clients came in. She threw the leash in my direction and told me to grab it so she could wash her hands. The lady demanded I take a paper towel and clean the leash off. I had to clean the poop off the leash for her because she couldn't manage. She was freaking out. I thought to myself, that's why there's soap, lady, but I didn't say anything."

Zoe continued. "We had this one client. She was the rudest with the poop. I remembered talking to her when she made an appointment. The appointment was for a vaccine so she could board her dog. As a courtesy, I told her that most boarding places also require a negative stool sample. I recommended she bring one of those in. I just wanted to give her a heads-up. The dog's vaccines weren't due yet, but the fecal test was overdue. I told her she could drop the stool sample off anytime. She didn't need an appointment.

"The woman came in the next day and chucked the bag of poop at me across the counter. She was visibly upset. I started entering the information in our system and told her the charge was thirty-three dollars.

"'I have an appointment in a several weeks,' she said. 'Can't I just pay then?'

"I said, 'We do require payment at time of services.'

"'You should have told me that. No one told me that! That's outrageous. I have to go to work right now and my wallet's out in the car. You expect me to go to my car and get it?'

"I told her that if she wanted us to check the stool that day, then yes. If she didn't have time, I said, she could stop by after work. The sample just needs to be within twenty-four hours. I explained that I'm required to collect payment before services.

"Her face turned red. She stormed out, and when she came back two minutes later, she chucked her wallet at me just like she had with the bag of poop. A big heavy wallet. I caught it before it hit me in the chest. Then she picked up the green bag of poop she had chucked at me before. I'd moved it to the far side of my desk but hadn't had a chance to run it to the back room yet.

"She picked up the bag of poop and slammed it down right in front of me. I'm lucky the bag didn't pop open."

Aunt Kae placed both of her hands over her mouth and laughed along with Tara. Zoe laughed only because she enjoyed seeing her mom and aunt laugh.

"Oh, my goodness. I can't believe people behave like that in a vet's office."

"That's only the tip of the iceberg," Tara said. "You wouldn't believe the work stories she tells. I'll grab some lemonade for us."

Kae nodded. "Lay another work story on me while your mom grabs the drinks."

Acknowledgments

My gratitude goes to Michelle Rayburn for her editing, cover design, typesetting, and guidance.

Special thanks to the Friends of the Pen writing group: Robin Steinweg, Anita Klumpers, and Joanie Shawhan. Thanks also to Sue Smith, who offered early editing advice. I'm privileged to call you my editors and friends. Your encouragement keeps me moving forward.

Thank you to my daughters, Paige and Sally, for sharing their lives and their stories with me.

I'm grateful to my dad for his consistent, unfailing support.

I also want to thank my everyday writing partners Robin Steinweg and Sandy Lipsky. Our daily accountability reports make a huge difference.

In addition, my gratitude goes to the *Turquoise Parade* launch team: Cindy Beard, Jean Crate, Shawn Pack, Sue Libey, Susan Flannagan, Cindy McWilliams, Karen Rothermel, Lien Polizzi, Susan Karsten, Vicky Dresser, Cheryl Brower, Michelle Sparks, Sepi Browning, Christy Williams, and Teresa White.

Finally, thank you to my husband, Mark, for his friendship and his support.

161

Dear Reader,

Thank you for taking the time to read *Turquoise Parade*. I hope you enjoyed the stories.

I have a favor to ask. Reviews are incredibly vital to writers. If you liked the book, I'd love it if you would post a review wherever you purchased *Turquoise Parade*.

If you'd like more short stories, you can join my mailing list on my website www.LoriLipsky.com. I'll send a bonus e-book to your inbox. You can also check out my first book, *Used Cookie Sheets*, a collection of forty-five very short stories.

Drop me a note at Lori@LoriLipsky.com. I enjoy hearing from readers.

All the best to you,

Lori Lipsky

Made in the USA
Columbia, SC
07 March 2022